Her breath came quick and shallow, and when she looked up and their eyes met...

Let me go, Lacey thought. *Let me go because we can't do this.*

Quinn's hand tightened until she was sure he had to feel her pulse hammering against his fingertips. "You've done nothing but help today. You even thought to pick up things for my daughter just in case, and you cooked for all of us, and I know you must hate having us intrude on your space..."

"It's fine—"

"...and the first chance I get I'm snapping at you."

"It's been a challenging day."

"And now you're making excuses for me. When what I should be doing is saying thank you."

She was certain her heart was going to beat clear through her chest when he pulled her closer and folded her in a hug.

Dear Reader,

When I was writing *The Cowboy's Christmas Gift*, I had a really hard time making sure I didn't give someone too much "screen time." That someone was Amber Solomon, the sweet little daughter of ranch manager Quinn Solomon. I just had to remind myself that Amber and Quinn would be able to share their story in the next book—this one, *The Cowboy's Valentine*.

The scenes with Amber seemed to write themselves. In many ways, it took me back a few years to when my own girls were little, with big eyes and gorgeous curls and an innocence that is both beautiful and heartbreaking. You see, Quinn's wife, Marie, died when Amber was very little, and it changed both of them forever.

Lacey Duggan has some wounds of her own to overcome, and I realized as the story unfolded that Lacey and Quinn and Amber all had the power to help heal each other's wounds. In the end, it was a really rewarding story to write, and one of my favorite happy-ever-afters.

Happy reading,

Donna

Suz
M.

THE COWBOY'S VALENTINE

DONNA ALWARD

Loved it!

HARLEQUIN® AMERICAN ROMANCE®

Recycling programs
for this product may
not exist in your area.

ISBN-13: 978-0-373-75556-1

The Cowboy's Valentine

Copyright © 2015 by Donna Alward

HARLEQUIN®
www.Harlequin.com

Printed in U.S.A.

A busy wife and mother of three (two daughters and the family dog), **Donna Alward** believes hers is the best job in the world: a combination of stay-at-home mom and romance novelist. An avid reader since childhood, Donna has always made up her own stories. She completed her arts degree in English literature in 1994, but it wasn't until 2001 that she penned her first full-length novel and found herself hooked on writing romance. In 2006 she sold her first manuscript, and now writes warm, emotional stories for Harlequin.

In her new home office in Nova Scotia, Donna loves being back on the east coast of Canada after nearly twelve years in Alberta, where her career began, writing about cowboys and the West. Donna's debut romance, *Hired by the Cowboy*, was awarded a Booksellers' Best Award in 2008 for Best Traditional Romance.

With the Atlantic Ocean only minutes from her doorstep, Donna has found a fresh take on life and promises even more great romances in the near future!

Donna loves to hear from readers. You can contact her through her website, donnaalward.com, or follow @DonnaAlward on Twitter.

Books by Donna Alward

Harlequin American Romance

Her Rancher Rescuer
The Texan's Baby
The Cowboy's Christmas Gift

Harlequin Romance

Honeymoon with the Rancher
A Family for the Rugged Rancher
How a Cowboy Stole Her Heart
The Last Real Cowboy
The Rebel Rancher
Sleigh Ride with the Rancher
Little Cowgirl on His Doorstep
A Cowboy To Come Home To
A Cadence Creek Christmas

Visit the Author Profile page at Harlequin.com for more titles.

Chapter One

The last place in the world Lacey Duggan expected to find herself was back at Crooked Valley Ranch.

It had only been a month since she'd shared the Christmas holiday with her brother Duke at the ranch they'd once called home. Those days were a lifetime ago. She'd never wanted to return to the small town of Gibson, Montana. Instead she'd made her life in Helena, working for the Department of Natural Resources and Conservation. She wasn't a farmer, or even much of an outdoor girl. Her work for the department was spent in an office. It wasn't that she didn't care; she genuinely enjoyed working with grant proposals and budgets. She just didn't need to be out there in hip waders or rubber boots doing all the digging around. The desk job suited her just fine.

Or at least it had. Past tense.

She stood on the porch of the main house, hesitating. All it would take was the slightest reach and she could open the door and step inside. But right now it seemed like too much to ask. The moment she did that was the moment she admitted every single aspect of her life had fallen apart. First it was the diagnosis that had killed her dreams. Then it was the divorce. She'd made it through both of those, holding on to what she had left—her job. Then came the kicker. The new budget had come down and her position had been made redundant. After six years in the same department, she was out of work.

And one-third owner of a ranch she didn't want.

A gust of wind swirled up the steps and around the porch, icy cold on her legs. This was ridiculous. It was just a door. It signified nothing, really. Except that it was warm in there and cold out here. With a frown she reached for the knob, only to have it ripped out of her hand the moment she touched it. She stared blindly as the door opened and a large figure stood in the doorway, blocking her from entering.

Quinn Solomon.

Her hand was still stretched out, hanging in thin air as she looked up to see the ranch manager staring down at her. Quinn. Quinn with the startling blue eyes and broad shoulders and long legs and cute daughter—and a low opinion of Lacey Duggan.

"Are you coming in or are you going to stand there all day?"

His harsh voice interrupted her assessment and despite the cold she felt her cheeks heat. "Sorry…"

"We're not paying to heat the outdoors. Get in here, you foolish woman."

Her pride blistered as she obeyed, sliding past him into the warmth of the foyer. The house wasn't huge but it was welcoming, and she dropped her purse on the floor and rubbed her arms a bit. Exactly how long had she stood out there?

She glanced up and met his probing gaze. "I didn't expect you to be here," she said, not meaning it to be an accusation, but it sounded like one just the same.

"I work here. My office is here. But don't worry, Lacey. I'll stay out of your way."

"I didn't mean it that way." She sighed. Duke and Quinn were good friends now, and she was sure her brother had told the ranch manager all about her situation, which was humiliating enough. "Look, Quinn, I'm not that happy about being here, either."

"I'm pretty sure I already knew that. So why *did* you come, Lacey?"

From the moment they'd met, he'd never beat around the bush with her. He always said exactly what was on his mind and she might have found that refreshing except that she was usually on the receiving end of a criticism. Her pride already smarting, she decided she'd meet bluntness with bluntness.

"The truth is, if I'd been wise and built up a better savings, I could have had cash flow to keep my place while I looked for another job. As it is, I had to cover my month's rent with my last paycheck and my unemployment won't kick in for another few weeks. My furniture is in my mom's garage while I figure things out, and I already feel like a big fat failure, so you don't have to go out of your way to exert your authority. I get it. You're the boss." She didn't even mention the car repair that had cost her nearly a thousand dollars. A thousand bucks might have at least afforded her a buffer. She couldn't seem to catch a break, and she'd die before going to Carter for money. She was pretty sure she was sick of the "throw good money after bad" speech.

He took a step closer, close enough that she could feel the warmth of his body emanating from beneath his plaid work shirt, smell the clean, fresh scent of his soap and see the particularly attractive bow shape to his lips. Determined, she stood her ground.

"This," he said darkly, "has absolutely nothing to do with my authority but a hell of a lot to do with yours. You own one-third of this ranch, but you've made it clear that you hate it and that it's a last resort for you. Forgive me if that doesn't make me feel all warm and fuzzy."

"I didn't mean it that way…"

He shook his head. "Yes, you did. And that's fine. Let's just not pretend it's anything other than what it is. You need a place that's free and Duke needs time to convince you to hang on to your third. My job? Is to run the place as if your family drama didn't exist."

She swallowed. He was absolutely right. Instead of appreciating the fact that she actually had an alternative, she was showing up with a big ol' resentful chip on her shoulder. It just so happened that Quinn seemed to be able to get her back up without even trying. He had from the moment they'd met.

"I don't want to keep you from your job, then," she replied, mollified. "I'll just get settled. And find Duke." She didn't know what would happen after that. She owned a third of Crooked Valley, but she knew absolutely nothing about running a ranch. What had her grandfather been thinking, anyway, leaving the place to the three of them? Duke had been in the Army when the will had been drafted, and Rylan…well, Rylan was never in one place for long. She supposed leaving the place to the three of them was the old man's way of getting them on the ranch since he hadn't succeeded in doing that when he was alive.

"Duke and Carrie are both out, moving the herd to a new pasture. They won't be in until midafternoon."

"Oh."

"You're a big girl. I'm sure you can find a way to amuse yourself. If you'll excuse me…"

She stepped aside, took off her coat and hung it on a hook in the entry. Quinn, on the other hand, pulled on boots, a heavy jacket, hat and thick gloves. "You'll find the door's rarely locked here, Lacey. All you have to do is turn the knob and come in."

It might have been a welcoming sort of sentiment if it hadn't made her feel stupid and foolish. With a huff she turned her back on Quinn and walked away, heading towards the kitchen and main living room. A few moments later she heard the door open and close and she finally relaxed her shoulders. Good riddance.

She had to admit, the house was cozy, despite its size. The downstairs contained a huge kitchen, living room, formal dining room, and the ranch office as well as a half bath and large doors exiting onto a deck that offered a view of rolling hills and the mountains in the distance. Upstairs, as she'd learned at Christmas, were four large bedrooms. All of them were vacant at the moment, though at Christmas they'd been partially occupied by her mom and stepdad, David, and her brother Rylan who'd surprised everyone by showing up. And for one night, Quinn had shared another with his daughter, Amber, who was a total sweetheart.

Lacey wondered if it mattered which room she took as hers during her stay. It was just temporary; there was no question of this being permanent. Maybe Duke thought he'd be able to convince her to take on her share, but Lacey had a plan. Sort of. She was going to take a few days off to refresh herself, and then she was going to spruce up her résumé and start applying for positions.

Surely someone needed a person with an accounting degree to do their accounts payable or something.

There were logs by the fireplace but it was unlit, so she took a few moments to set up some kindling and light a match. It took a while for the dry wood to catch, but when it did Lacey was pleased with herself. She'd check the fridge, maybe make some coffee or tea and chill in front of the fire for this afternoon. She added a stick of wood to the growing flames and wished she'd worn a thicker sweater. Which reminded her that she hadn't brought in her bags...

A loud thump startled her, making her jump as she pressed her hand to her heart. The door opened down the hall, followed by stomping of feet and a general commotion. When she stepped around the corner, she saw two of her suitcases standing guard at the bottom of the stairs, and Quinn's retreating back as he went to her car a second time, retrieving her last suitcase and an overnight bag.

She wished he'd just left it alone. She didn't want to be beholden to him for anything. Ever.

He stomped in again and put down the bags. "Your hatchback was unlocked. I saw the bags through the window, and..."

"Thank you, Quinn. I was just going to get them. I appreciate you bringing them in."

Her polite voice seemed to take him off guard and he stared at her for a moment. "You're welcome."

The civil exchange made for an uncomfortable silence between them. A log snapped on the fire and he raised his eyebrows. "You built a fire?"

"It was a little chilly in here. I thought I'd make some tea, get settled, that sort of thing."

"Right." He lifted a finger to his hat. "Well, I'll be off. I'll be in the horse barn if you need anything, and by the time I take off for the day, Duke will be back."

"You have to pick up Amber at day care," she supplied, smiling a little. It was hard not to smile when thinking about the little chatterbox—even if it did cause a pang of sadness in Lacey's heart. It was totally unfair that Amber was left without a mother and Quinn without his wife. By all accounts, Marie Solomon had doted on her child and been a perfect mom. Something Lacey would never be.

"Yeah. Anyway, I'd better go. Work won't do itself."

She shut the door behind him, then scooted to the office window and watched him walk across the yard, long strides eating up the distance between the house and the barn. He'd touched his hat, such an old-fashioned, mannerly gesture, that she was momentarily nonplussed. She wasn't sure they even made men like that anymore. Certainly Carter had never been like that. Not unless there'd been an audience, and then he'd been all chivalry and sweetness. But when they were alone? The walls went up between them again. By the time they'd divorced, she'd been relieved—even if she did still blame herself for how it all went wrong. She'd held on too tight, fought too hard and driven him away.

Then again, there was a limit to Quinn's chivalry. He hadn't offered to carry her bags upstairs, had he? Just put them inside the door and expected her to get on with it. She was glad. She was a big girl and could look after herself. Including making a few trips up and down stairs to transport her luggage.

She was huffing and puffing by the time the last bag was settled in what she assumed was the master bedroom. The heavy pine furniture was solid and sturdy, the quilt on the top she suspected was homemade—perhaps by her grandmother, Eileen? She was a little sad that she didn't know, that the connection to the Duggan side of the family had faltered so much after Lacey's father's death. All in all, this was her new temporary home and she felt like a square peg in a round hole.

But she'd make the best of it. She always rallied after being kicked around, and this time was no different. She sat on the bed, fell back into the soft covers, and stared at the ceiling, wondering exactly where she should start.

QUINN HAD KNOWN she was arriving today. He'd thought it would be later, that he'd finish his work in the house and be gone outside by the time she arrived and they could avoid that awkward first meeting. Lacey Duggan had every right to be at Crooked Valley—she owned a third of it.

It was the fact that she didn't value it that got under his skin. She'd rather sell the place and be rid of it entirely. The only reason she hadn't pushed for that solution to the inheritance dilemma left by her grandfather, Joe, was that Duke had come home first and wanted to make a go of it. The whole family looked at Duke as some hero…a military vet with a permanent hearing disability who stepped in when everything went wrong.

Quinn had been skeptical, but he'd liked Duke right away. Humble and not afraid to admit he didn't know what he was doing. Willing to learn and work. Ready to lead.

But Lacey? That woman had waltzed in here at Thanksgiving and come right out and told Duke that he should unload the place. As if it and the people who worked it and loved it meant nothing.

Things had to be really desperate for her to agree to move in for a while.

He opened the front door to Sunshine Smiles Day Care and let his troubles drift away. It smelled like sugar cookies and fruit punch and there were happy squeals coming from the playroom. He smiled at the young woman at the front. "Hey, Melanie."

"Hey, yourself. Amber's helping clean up from after-school snacks. I'll get her."

His daughter was the light of his life. She attended preschool for half days and spent the balance of the day at the day care. There were times he felt guilty about the amount of time she spent with people other than a parent, but it couldn't be helped. Being a single dad was a hard job. He'd had to get good at things like pigtails and bows. There'd been a lot of tears before he got a handle on the tiny elastics and learned how to make a bow so that the ribbons didn't sag and droop. Marie had always done the little girly things. She'd known Amber's favorite colors, foods and preferred toys, sang to her at night and read her favorite stories. It wasn't that Quinn hadn't been involved—of course he had. But Marie had been the anchor. The details person, the one who held them all together.

He still missed her every damn day. And not just for the details and day-to-day jobs he'd had to assume. He missed having someone to laugh with, missed hearing her breathing when she slept, her voice when she called out for him to do something, the way she ran her hands through his hair. He was damned lonely and struggling to get through every day.

"Daddy!"

He smiled suddenly as Amber came charging out of the playroom. "Hey, princess! How was school?"

"It was good. We gots to paint pictures of our favorite thing to do in winter."

He knew what hers was, but he asked anyway. "And what did you paint?"

She twirled in a circle. "Skating!"

Quinn's skating expertise was limited to hockey skates and a pond scrimmage now and again. This year Amber had wanted to learn, so for Christmas he'd bought her little white figure skates and signed her up for weekly lessons at the rink in town.

"Nice," he commented, reaching for her backpack while she shoved her arms in her coat. "Come on, let's go home and get some supper on."

She was jamming her hat on her head as she peered up at him. "Can we go see Duke and Carrie? I want to show them my picture."

"Maybe another time." Quinn swallowed, thinking about Lacey being at the house by herself tonight. She'd looked sort of...lost, he thought. It didn't really matter that he wasn't overly fond of her. Losing your job was stressful, especially when you didn't have a backup plan. She'd been making ends meet on a mediocre salary. He knew how upset he'd be if he lost his job and had Amber to support.

Maybe he was being too hard on Lacey.

"Please, Daddy? I haven't seen Duke all week." She pouted prettily as she took his hand and they walked to the door.

"Duke was still out in the pasture when I left. He might not even be back yet. Maybe tomorrow."

"Okay."

He helped her buckle into her booster seat in the back-seat of his truck and then got in and started the engine. "Hey, pumpkin? Do you remember Lacey, Duke's sister? The one that was here for Thanksgiving and Christmas?"

He looked in the rearview mirror. Amber was nodding vigorously. "The pretty lady," she announced. "With the long red hair. Like Ariel."

Quinn blinked. He wasn't sure that Lacey looked like Ariel from *The Little Mermaid*, but there was no question that she had gorgeous hair—when she didn't have it all pulled off her face and shoved into a tail or bun or braid. He'd only seen it down once, but Amber had hit the nail on the head. Her hair was long and thick, a rich burnished color with just a hint of natural wave. Even disheveled in the morning, as he'd seen her on Christmas Eve, it was stunning.

"Daddy? What about her?"

He was pulled back from his musings. "Oh," he replied, turning at a stop sign. "Just that she's going to be staying at the big house for a while. I know I take you with me a lot, so when you're there you're going to have to be extra good. It's not just you and me now."

"But Lacey is nice. She played with me lots."

"But she might not want to entertain you all the time, sweetheart. Do you understand?"

Amber shrugged. He could see the exaggerated movement in the rearview mirror and his heart gave a sad little thump again. The gesture was so like Marie. Amber had parts of Marie that she didn't even realize, because her memories of her mother were already beginning to dim. They should have had Marie longer. She should have been here through all of this. They were like a jigsaw puzzle with pieces missing. Pieces that could never be replaced.

"How about spaghetti for supper?" he asked, suggesting one of Amber's favorites. There had to be at least one more container of frozen sauce in the freezer. It wouldn't take long to thaw it and cook some noodles and throw some garlic bread in the oven. Cooking was something else he'd learned to do over the past year and a half.

"Spaghetti! Yum! I'll help!"

He smiled then, pushing the maudlin thoughts aside. He might miss Marie, but he was still a lucky man. He had a job he loved, a roof over his head and a daughter he adored. They could muddle through the rest if they had each other.

Lacey, on the other hand, would be sitting at the ranch house tonight all alone. And for the first time, he truly felt sorry for her.

Chapter Two

Lacey was up, showered, and dressed by the time Quinn arrived just before eight. She'd made a point of setting the alarm for six-thirty, though it hadn't mattered. She'd awakened shortly after five, cold, and had thrown another quilt over top of the blankets in an effort to warm up. By six she gave up trying to go back to sleep and got up, cranked up the heat and ran a hot shower.

Now she had her laptop open, a cup of coffee beside her, and her glasses perched on her nose when she heard the truck drive in and the door slam.

There was a knock on the door.

Frowning, she got up to answer it. Maybe it wasn't Quinn arriving for the day? When she put her eye up to the peephole, she could see his scowly face on the other side. What the heck?

She opened the door. "Quinn. Why on earth did you knock?"

He stepped inside, bringing a gust of icy air with him. "You live here now. I don't have any desire to walk in and take you by surprise."

Her face heated as the possibilities of "surprise" sank in. "Well." She took a step backward as he toed off his boots. "Thanks, but this place is really more yours than mine." She realized they needed to set some boundaries with each other and it might as well start this morning. "Tell you what. During work hours, this place is yours. You should be able to come and go as you please and not worry about knocking."

"It's a ranch, Lacey. Not exactly a nine-to-five job."

Did he always have to be so contrary?

"I realize that. But you have to admit, most days you come and go at regular hours. Let's say…between eight and six, you've got free run of the place and I'll work around you. The rest of the time, it just takes a knock. Okay?"

He gave a short nod. "Okay."

She smiled. "Good. Now, do you want some coffee? I put on a pot and I shouldn't drink the whole thing or I'll be bouncing off the walls by noon."

He looked surprised that she'd asked, and his face relaxed a little. "That would be good."

"What do you take in it?"

"Cream and sugar."

Same as her. Go figure.

She retrieved a mug from a cupboard while he put a lunch bag in the fridge. When he turned around he noticed her laptop on the dining table. "What are you working on so early?" he asked, accepting the steaming mug from her hands. The pads of his fingers brushed against her knuckles.

She withdrew quickly, alarmed that the thoughtless touch felt so intimate. "I'm sprucing up my résumé. Then I'll log on to the Wi-Fi and start searching the job sites and boards. I'm a CPA. Surely someone between here and Great Falls could use my considerable accounting skills." She waggled her eyebrows, trying to keep the mood light. Maybe he could at least give her points for trying.

"I could ask around."

Another surprise. "Why would you do that?"

He took a sip of his coffee and looked at her over the rim of his cup. "The faster you get a job, the faster you can resume your old life."

The whisper of intimacy disintegrated. "Harsh."

"We both know you don't really want to live here, Lacey. No sense pretending otherwise."

He was right. But it didn't mean she hated it entirely. "You realize that you give me crap for judging ranch life but you do the exact same thing with me? You're just as prejudiced, you know."

Quinn looked slightly alarmed at that assessment and put his coffee cup on the island. "What?"

"I'm just saying, that sure, I've made it no secret that this is not the life I'd choose for myself. But you're judging me for that. Quinn, I respect that this is your home and your livelihood and you like it. But just because it's not for me, and I know it, doesn't make me less than you, okay?"

He stared at her for a long moment. "I just got schooled," he admitted. "You're right. I shouldn't judge. You just…"

"Drive you crazy?"

"Yeah."

"You push my buttons, too." Their gazes connected and that strange intimate feeling happened again. She swallowed. "It must be because we're so different. Oil and water."

"I'm sure that's it."

Another heavy silence. Finally Quinn picked up his

cup. "I need to make a few calls before heading out again. And you look like you need to get back to your work. I'll see you later."

"Sure." She folded her arms around her middle, still a bit chilly. "Quinn, one more thing. Do you always keep it so cold in here? I woke up at five this morning darn near freezing."

He stopped at the entrance to the hall. "I never thought about that. We keep the thermostat turned down, just keep enough heat on to keep pipes from freezing, really. I use a space heater in the office."

"I don't mind turning the heat down at night, though maybe not that far down." She briefly considered an electric blanket, but that wouldn't solve the entire problem. And she didn't want to blast the heat in the whole house and run up a huge bill.

"I'll speak to Duke about it, maybe get some programmable thermostats," Quinn promised. "In the meantime, do you want me to light a fire for you?"

"I can do it. And I turned up the heat in these rooms anyway. Forget I mentioned it."

He walked away to his office and she resumed her seat at the table. Even with the heat on, she was glad she'd put on warm leggings and the long sweater. Her coffee was gone before long so she got up and refilled her cup then went back to it.

She was just prettying up her margins and spacing when she looked up and saw Quinn at the end of the hallway, putting on his outerwear. He didn't realize she was watching, and she let her eyes roam over his long, strong legs and wide shoulders as he put on his boots and jacket. Then his hat and a heavy pair of gloves… and her mouth watered.

Maybe they did get along about as well as cats in a sack. But she was still woman enough to appreciate a fine male form and it was hard to find fault with Quinn's.

She hurriedly glanced down at her monitor as Quinn looked back towards the kitchen. It wouldn't do to get caught staring. They could hardly agree on anything. Heck, at Christmastime they'd argued about the correct way to mash potatoes, for heaven's sake. If he had the smallest inkling she found him physically attractive… well, things were already super awkward around here.

"I'll be back in later to grab my lunch," he called, and he was out the door before she could reply.

Surly, she thought. That was the problem with Quinn Solomon. He was surly. It was hard to like a man who hardly ever smiled.

She wondered if he'd smiled more before his wife had died, and her heart turned over a little at the thought. Whether she liked him or not, losing his wife and the mother of his daughter had to be terribly sad. He must have loved her a lot…

She and Carter hadn't had that sort of love. She'd thought they had, at first. But when put to the test, they didn't have what it took for a successful marriage.

She pushed her glasses up her nose and focused on the spacing of her résumé. There was no sense worrying about a past that couldn't be changed. The only thing she could do was look to the future. There were days when even that was difficult, but she had a clean start now. It was up to her to make the most of it.

She was in the middle of bookmarking employment sites where she could upload her CV when Duke blustered in. Without knocking. Ah. Big brothers. Funny. When Quinn had knocked, Lacey had felt *she* was imposing on *him*. When her brother entered without knocking, his sense of entitlement got on her nerves a little.

"You made it." He shrugged off his coat and hung it on the hook.

"Yesterday, as a matter of fact. Thanks for noticing." She sent him a cheeky grin, making sure to face him straight on. Duke's hearing was compromised, and he often watched lips to fill in any gaps of clarity, especially if his head was turned a bit the wrong way.

"I was going to come over last night, but Carrie and I didn't finish until late. By the time supper was over, we were tuckered out." He'd removed his boots and came into the kitchen in his stocking feet. His face got this weird, soft, moony look about it. "Especially Carrie. I keep telling her not to overdo it, but she's stubborn."

Lacey liked Carrie a lot. The former foreman of the cattle operation, Carrie had fallen for Duke hard and fast when he'd come back to Crooked Valley. Now she and Duke were married and she was expecting his baby. Duke was so happy and protective, and Lacey was happy for them. Even so, their happiness and future plans did serve as a painful reminder of the life she would never have. The dream of an adoring husband and a house full of kids was long gone.

"Is Carrie feeling okay?" Lacey sat back in her chair and took off her glasses, putting them on top of her paper tablet.

"The odd morning sickness, but nothing major. And she's tired a lot. Otherwise, she's great." He pulled out a chair and sat down, resting his elbows on the table. "I can't wait for the ultrasound. We'll get pictures and everything."

It was like a knife to the heart, but Lacey never let

on. No one except their mother knew that Lacey'd had to undergo surgery—the kind that prevented her from ever having children.

"I'm glad you're so happy." That, at least, was the truth.

"And you're here. That makes me happy." He grinned at her, his blue eyes sparkling at her. "I always love having a little sis around to torment."

"Don't get your hopes up. I appreciate the place to stay, but I'm not really interested in becoming a rancher. Gramps was crazy to split this place up the way he did."

Duke tapped his fingers on the table. "I used to think that, too."

"Well, you're not me. I'm not a rancher. I belong behind a desk somewhere, working with columns of numbers. Not shoveling manure or whatever it is you guys do outside all day."

Duke laughed. "I forgot you're such a girlie girl."

"Yes, well, you haven't exactly been around much the last few years." She realized that sounded a bit harsh, so she tempered it a little. "You were deployed, Duke. I don't blame you in the least. But you must realize that life went on while you were overseas. We all went our own ways."

She let him off the hook and smiled. "Anyway, I do really want to say thank-you for letting me crash. Losing my job was a big blow. I was living paycheck to paycheck and really couldn't see how I could keep up with the rent on the town house."

"What about Carter? Doesn't he pay you any alimony?"

She nodded. "Yes, but it's not much. Carter's alimony

is peanuts, really. He's got his own troubles. I wouldn't ask him for anything more."

"You'd be within your rights. He walked out on you and left you with everything—including all the debt."

As Lacey thought about how to answer her brother, she got up and poured him the last cup of coffee from the pot. She put it down in front of him and then put her hand on his shoulder.

"It was a mutual decision, Duke," she said softly. "It just wasn't working. We were both unhappy." She didn't feel like mentioning that the debt Duke spoke of was mostly due to her and all her medical tests and treatment that weren't covered by her insurance. "I just want you to know that I appreciate the chance to stay here while I figure out what's next."

Duke smiled down into his coffee.

"What?"

He looked up and his eyes crinkled around the edges. "You sound like me a few months ago."

She knew Duke wanted her to take on her third of the ranch. If she did, and if they could convince Rylan to take on his third, the ranch stayed as is. But if they didn't...well, Duke would either have to find a way to buy them out of their thirds, or the place would be sold. It was an annoying thing, what their grandfather had done in his will. And it would have been much easier to brush off if Duke hadn't decided to stay on.

"I'm not taking on my third, Duke. I'll help you in any way I can, but not that."

Duke took a long drink of his cooling coffee. "Well, there's lots of time to think about it. What are you doing today?"

His whole dismissal sent out a message of "give me

time to change your mind" and she ignored it. "I'm sending out my résumé, seeing if I can find any leads to a new job. It's not an ideal commute to Great Falls, but spring will be here soon and the bad weather is mostly done. I can do it for a while, until I build up some financial reserves. And who knows? Maybe I'll find something closer."

"Have you seen Quinn yet?"

She raised an eyebrow. "Of course I did. He was the welcoming committee." She smiled saucily.

"Oh, great. You weren't too hard on him, were you?"

She gave him a swat. "So much for family loyalty. What about how grouchy he might have been to me?"

Duke's frown deepened. "Was he?"

"Of course not." No matter her issues with Quinn, she wouldn't put Duke in the middle of it. He relied on Quinn too much. She wasn't here to stir up trouble.

"Hey. If I had one reservation about you staying at the house, it was that you'd be sharing space with Quinn. I know you don't get along. I don't know why, but you don't. I'm hoping you can coexist peacefully."

"We've laid out some ground rules." She sat back down at the table.

"Well, try not to kill each other. This place doesn't run without him." Duke raised his cup, drained what was left of his coffee, and stood. "Thanks for the coffee. I'd better get back."

"Anytime. This is your place, after all."

"No, it's yours. For as long as you want it, Lace." He put his hand over hers on top of the table. "I mean that. I wasn't around a lot, definitely not when you were going through some rough times. I'd like to be there for you now."

The backs of her eyes stung and she nodded through blurred vision. "That means a lot, Duke."

"Right. Better be off." He went down the hall and put on his gear again. "Oh, Lace?"

She looked up.

"Maybe next time you can have some cookies to go with that coffee? Carrie's on a 'no sweets' kick with the pregnancy. And somehow her kale chips just aren't cutting it for me."

She couldn't help but smile. "I'll see what I can do," she replied. "Now go, so I can find a job, will you?"

With a wink he disappeared.

Lacey turned her attention back to the document on the screen but didn't really focus on it. Instead she was thinking about what Duke had just said, and thinking about how it felt to be here. It felt good. It felt…right. Somehow being with family, having that support, was exactly what she needed.

She just had to be careful not to get too used to it, or use it as a crutch. This time she was making her own decisions and standing entirely on her own two feet. At least if she relied on herself, she wasn't being set up for disappointment.

JACK, ONE OF the regular hands, was out with the flu so Quinn spent the rest of his morning mucking out stalls in the horse barn. It was a job he actually enjoyed. The slight physical exertion kept him warm and he usually talked to the horses as he worked. Even the scrape of the shovel on the barn floor had a comforting sound to it, and he worked away with the radio playing in the background, just him and his thoughts.

He had a lot of thoughts, as it happened. Most days it

was about what needed to be done at the ranch, or worries about being a good single dad to Amber as she got older. He already knew far more about Disney princesses and ballet slippers and hair ribbons than most dads. And it wasn't that he minded. It was just...he knew Marie would have done a much better job. A little girl needed a mom. And Quinn wasn't sure how to solve that, because he wasn't really interested in getting married again.

Not when it had hurt so much the first time.

Thankfully he had Carrie and Kailey. Carrie was around even more now that she and Duke were married, and Amber loved spending time at Crooked Valley. Kailey was Carrie's best friend and lived at a neighboring ranch. Between the two of them, they provided Amber with some great girlie time. On Sundays, too, they visited with Quinn's mom, who lived in a little one-bedroom apartment in Great Falls. She'd moved there after his dad had died and she had a vital, happy life in the assisted-living complex, and help with the arthritis that sometimes made her day-to-day living a challenge.

Visits and special time were great. The girls were great. But they weren't her mother, and Quinn couldn't help but feel like he'd somehow let Amber down even though Marie's death had been a freak accident. A heart defect that had gone undetected until it was too late. One morning she'd been laughing with him over breakfast. Two hours later she'd just been...gone.

At noon he ventured back to the house and lifted his hand to knock at the door, then pulled it back again. Lacey had said to come and go as he pleased, and he should. This was, after all, a working ranch. He was pretty sure she wasn't going to be running around the house in her Skivvies at twelve o'clock in the afternoon.

The thought gave him pause, because he pictured her that way and his body tensed in a familiar way. Oh, no. That would be too inconvenient. He had no business thinking about Lacey Duggan in her underwear and even less business liking it.

He reached for the doorknob and resolutely turned it. He stepped into the foyer and heard a radio playing, heard a soft female voice singing along. He was transported back two years earlier, when he'd still had the perfect life, and the joy he felt coming home to a scene much like this one. There was the sound of something opening and closing, and the rattle of bake ware. The aroma of fresh-baked cookies reached him and his stomach growled in response.

After hanging up his coat, he wandered to the kitchen to get his lunch out of the fridge. He'd just go eat in the office, out of Lacey's way. It was a lonely-sounding proposition but he realized that if he stayed in her little sphere of existence, they'd probably end up arguing. They always did.

"Don't mind me. I'm just here to get my lunch."

He forgot that she had music on. That she probably hadn't heard him come inside. But he remembered now as she squeaked and jumped with alarm, jerking the spatula which held a perfectly round, warm, chocolate chip cookie. The cookie went flying and landed with a soft splat in the middle of the kitchen floor.

"Cripes, Quinn!" Her brows pulled together in annoyance. "Do you have to creep up on a person like that?"

She looked so indignant he had the strangest urge to laugh. "I wasn't trying to be quiet. I came in like I always do. I guess you didn't hear me because of the music."

"Whatever." She bent to pick up the cookie, which

broke into pieces as she lifted it off the floor. She put the remnants on the counter and then went for a piece of paper towel to wipe the little dots of melted chocolate from the tile.

Quinn went to the fridge and took out his lunch bag. "Well, if it's any consolation, they smell great."

He turned around and headed back towards the hall.

"Where are you going?"

He paused and looked over his shoulder. "I was going to eat in the office."

"Is that where you normally eat?"

He didn't know how to answer. He usually grabbed his lunch, made himself a coffee, used the microwave if he had leftovers to heat. Today he had leftover spaghetti, which he'd planned to eat cold.

"I assume your lack of a fast reply means no. You normally use the kitchen, don't you?"

He sighed. "Sometimes."

"Truly, Quinn, I don't want you to alter your routine for me. Pretend I'm not here."

It was pretty hard to pretend because she was there, with her burnished curls caught up in a ponytail, her blue eyes snapping at him. He noticed, not for the first time, that she had the faintest dusting of freckles over the bridge of her nose. Duke was thirty, so that had to make her, what, twenty-eight or so?

Twenty-eight, with a career job behind her, married, divorced. Quinn was thirty-three, and he knew exactly how life could age a person so that numbers were insignificant. He tried to remember that Lacey had faced her share of troubles. Duke had made it plain that the family wasn't too impressed that her ex had walked out on her.

He went back and put his lunch bag on the island, unzipped it and took out the plastic container holding his lunch. "Do you mind if I use the microwave?"

She rolled her eyes. "What did I just say?"

Saucy. At least she was consistent.

He popped the container in the microwave and started it up, then stood awkwardly waiting for it to beep. Meanwhile, Lacey finished removing the cookies from the pan and began dropping batter by the spoonful on the parchment.

His stomach growled again.

When his meal was hot, he took it to the kitchen table—no laptop in sight now—and got out his knife and fork. The pasta didn't look as appetizing as it might have. He was an adequate cook only, but he was getting better. Trying new things now and again. The trouble was that by the time he got Amber from day care, he had to cook stuff that was relatively fast if they hoped to eat before her bath time.

He was nearly through when Lacey put a small plate beside him and a glass of milk.

"Uh, thanks," he said, looking up. She was smiling down at him, and for the first time there was no attitude in her expression.

"I'd be pretty heartless if I didn't offer you fresh cookies," she said. "Besides, I don't dare eat them all myself. I'm counting on you and Duke to eat the lion's share."

She went back to the sink and ran soapy water to wash the dishes.

Quinn bit into a cookie and sighed in appreciation. God, the woman knew how to cook. He'd realized that at Thanksgiving and then again at Christmas when she'd bustled in with all her bossiness. He and Amber had both enjoyed the home-cooked meals they'd shared here at the ranch. It had actually stung his pride a little when Amber asked if they could go back to "Uncle Duke's" because Lacey was there and doing a lot of the family cooking along with their mother, Helen.

"They turn out okay?" Lacey called from the sink, her hands immersed in the water. "I didn't have my recipe with me and went from memory."

He bit back a sarcastic comment. Why did she push his buttons so? Instead he reminded himself that she'd gone out of her way to be nice. To be accommodating. "They're delicious," he replied honestly. "Maybe the best chocolate chip cookie I've ever had."

She dried her hands on a dish towel, then grabbed a cookie and her coffee cup and joined him at the table. "Can I tell you a secret, Quinn?"

They were sharing confidences now?

"Um, sure. I guess."

She bit into the cookie, chewed thoughtfully and swallowed. "I bake when I'm stressed. I think it's a combination of things, from focusing on something other than what's going on, to the process of making something and maybe even the aromas. They're comforting smells, you know?"

He did know. He missed them around his place, and the absence of them sometimes made his chest ache.

"You're stressed?"

She broke off another piece of cookie. "Of course I am. Know what they said when I packed up my desk at the office? 'Oh, no, who's going to bring us treats all the time?' I mean, it's been better up until a few months ago, but when Carter first left…"

Right. Carter. That was the bastard's name.

"When Carter left it was weird, being all alone. We'd planned to be together forever, you know?"

His last bite of cookie swelled in his throat as a heavy silence fell over the table.

"Oh, God," she whispered, and to his surprise she put her hand on his arm. "I'm so sorry. That was so thoughtless of me. Of course you know."

He forced the cookie down and looked up at her. Her eyes were soft with sympathy and understanding and her hand was still on his wrist. Something passed between them, something that, for a flash, felt like shared grief. It was gone in the blink of an eye, but it had been there. He got the feeling that she understood more than he realized. Still, could divorce be as bad as a spouse dying? As bad as a child without a mother?

Lacey pulled her hand away. "I'm sorry," she repeated. "It's been so quiet here that I've talked your ear off. I should let you get back to work."

He cleared his throat. "Yes. Thanks for the cookies."

"Anytime. They'll be in Grandma Duggan's cookie jar if you find yourself snackish." She gestured towards a stone crock that she must have unearthed from somewhere, now sitting on the counter next to the toaster.

"Will do."

Quinn put the lid on his dish and shoved everything back in his lunch bag, then put it in the fridge, empty, where he'd collect it at the end of the day.

Back in the office he pulled up a spreadsheet and tried to wrap his mind around the numbers in the columns, but nothing was fitting together right. His focus was shot. He kept getting stuck on the look on Lacey's face when she admitted she using baking as a coping mechanism. She'd looked lonely. Vulnerable. Feelings he could relate to so easily that when she'd put her fingers on his sleeve, he'd been tempted to turn his hand over and link his fingers with hers.

Ludicrous. Crazy. Duke Duggan's sister, for Pete's sake. His boss's pain-in-the-butt sister who hated anything to do with ranching.

With a frown he tweaked the column again, fixing the formula at the end. It wouldn't do to start thinking of Lacey Duggan in a friendly way. Certainly not in a kindred spirits kind of way.

A few hours later he heard her go out the door, heard her start her car and drive away. He let out a breath. Working here while Lacey was living at the house was going to be tougher than he thought—and not for the reasons he expected.

She wasn't back yet when he got his lunch bag from the fridge and left to pick up Amber. But when he got home, and as supper was cooking, he opened the bag to take out his dirty dishes. To his surprise, the container that had held his lunch was perfectly clean, and a little bag was beside it, full of cookies. A sticky note was stuck to the front. "For you and Amber," it said.

Quinn swallowed. Lacey had to stop being so nice, trying so hard. She was going to make it difficult for him to keep disliking her if she kept it up.

Chapter Three

Lacey had only been at Crooked Valley three days when she got her first phone call, asking her for an interview. A company in Great Falls was looking for someone to do their payroll. When Quinn came in for lunch on the day of the interview, she was running a lint brush over the dark material of a straight skirt. For some reason little bits of fluff kept sticking to the fabric, and she wanted to look perfect.

Her head told her it was just an interview at a manufacturing company, not a high-powered lawyer's office or anything. Neat and tidy business wear would have sufficed, but she was determined to put her absolute best foot forward. She'd brought out the big guns: black pencil skirt, cream silk blouse, patent heels.

She was turning into the kitchen from the downstairs bath at the same time as Quinn entered from the hall. Both of them stopped short, but Quinn just stared at her. "Oh. Hi." He sort of recovered from the surprise but his expression plumped up her confidence just a little. It was definitely approval that glowed in his eyes for the few seconds before he shuttered it away.

"I have an interview this afternoon," she said, grabbing some hand lotion from the windowsill above the sink. She rubbed it into her hands as Quinn opened the fridge. "In Great Falls."

"That's good news," he answered, but now she noticed he was avoiding looking at her.

She frowned. Maybe she'd misread his expression before. "Do I look all right, Quinn? Should I maybe wear a different top or something? Are pearls a little too much?" She touched the strand at her collarbone. They were her grandmother Eileen's pearls. As the only granddaughter, they'd automatically gone to her. She rarely wore them, but it seemed appropriate somehow now that Lacey was living in the farmhouse. Like a good luck charm.

"You look fine," he answered.

Her frown deepened. He hadn't looked up when he said it, just stuck his lunch in the microwave and set the timer.

"I was hoping for something more than fine. More like, 'Wow, let's hire this one on the spot.'"

He turned and looked at her then, his face set in an impersonal mask. "You look great, Lacey. Very professional." He paused. "Very pretty."

It might have meant more if it didn't seem as if it pained him to say it.

"Thanks," Lacey replied, and then felt a bit silly. She hadn't really been fishing for a compliment, but it felt that way now.

She wanted a splash of color, so she transferred her wallet and necessary items from her black purse to a turquoise handbag. "I made a coffee cake this morning," she said, doing a check for her car keys. "It's under the domed lid. Help yourself."

The microwave dinged and Quinn took out his lunch. "You trying to fatten me up with all this baking?"

"Not much chance of that." The words came out before she could think. She'd noticed Quinn's build. A little on the slim side, and she wondered if it was because he found it hard to work and be a full-time dad and do all the household things that needed to be done. "Like I said, I enjoy doing it. And I don't really have anyone to cook for. Duke's started coming in for coffee break each morning, and sometimes Carrie comes with him, but she's really watching her diet with the baby and all." Once again, the little pang of envy touched her heart but she pushed it away.

She'd never have a big family to cook for. She might as well accept it.

She took a minute and looked at Quinn. Really looked at him, and wondered what it must be like to lose a spouse and try to raise a small child on your own. Certainly he was doing a good job, but at what cost? She noticed he didn't smile all that often, and his eyes had lines at the corners. He wasn't that old, either. Maybe midthirties at the most. It seemed more like life had aged him.

"Quinn, how's Amber doing?"

He shrugged and twirled some spaghetti noodles on his fork. "She's fine. Likes preschool. Does okay at the day care."

"It must be rough, bringing her up on your own."

He looked up at her sharply. "We get by."

"Oh, of course you do. I just thought that..." She hesitated. What was she thinking, anyway? She didn't really want to get involved with Quinn's life, did she? They'd sort of formed a truce since she'd moved in. Less criticizing and arguing, and that was good. Still slightly awkward, but good.

Truth of the matter was, Lacey was lonely. She didn't

know anyone in Gibson, didn't have contact with colleagues since she was out of work, and she was going just a little bit stir-crazy here at Crooked Valley.

"I just thought that since cooking for one is a real pain, maybe I could send some food home with you. It's stupid. I make a recipe and then end up either freezing or throwing out half because it's more than I can eat."

"Didn't you cook for one before?"

She did, but it was different. "To be honest? I froze some, and I often gave some to a neighbor. She was elderly and alone and struggled to cook for herself and eat enough."

Quinn's eyes snapped at her. "So what, Amber and I look like we need charity, is that it?"

"No!" She twisted her fingers together. "I didn't mean that."

"We get along just fine, thanks." His lips were set, and Lacey dropped the subject. She hadn't meant to insult him or imply he was, well, lacking in any area.

"I'd better get going, then," she said quietly, and picked up her handbag.

"Good luck. I hope you get it," he answered, but his voice lacked any warmth and the encouragement stung. Sure he hoped she got it, so she'd be out of his hair. Message received loud and clear.

She reached for her coat and keys and left him sitting there at the table. Maybe he was lonely and bitter but she didn't have to be! She was starting a new chapter in her life, and Quinn Solomon was not going to bring her down.

But fate had other ideas that afternoon. The directions that had seemed so clear earlier were suddenly not, and she got turned around. It was five minutes after her scheduled appointment time when she pulled into the parking lot. In her rush, she snagged her panty hose getting out of the car and there was no time to change or take them off, just hope that it wouldn't be visible once she was seated.

She stopped outside the office door, blew out a breath, rolled her shoulders, pasted on a smile and walked in.

"Hi," she greeted the receptionist. "I'm Lacey Duggan, here for the interview?"

The receptionist looked at her over the top of her glasses. "Just have a seat for a minute. Can I get you anything? Coffee?"

If she were any more hyped up she'd explode. "Maybe some water? That'd be great."

The woman returned with a small glass of water. Lacey removed her coat and hung it on a nearby coat tree and she reminded herself to calm down. It had only been a few days. This was her first interview. She took a sip of water and at the same time, her cell phone buzzed in the purse on her lap. It startled her enough that she jumped, and splashed water on the front of her silk blouse.

For the love of Mike.

An office door opened just as she was reaching in her bag for her phone. She dropped it back into the purse and stood up as a friendly-looking woman came out and smiled at her. She would get herself together and ignore her bad luck so far...

"You must be Ms. Duggan. I'm Corinna Blackwood. We spoke on the phone yesterday." She held out her hand and Lacey shook it.

The head of HR. And she looked approachable. Maybe Lacey could turn this around.

"I tried to call you about an hour ago," Ms. Blackwood said, stepping back. "I'm sorry you drove all this way. We filled the position earlier this afternoon."

Lacey swallowed, so surprised she didn't know how to respond. "I see." She licked her lips and tried not to sigh. "I drove in from Gibson. I must have just missed you."

"Yes, I spoke to someone at your home number. He said he'd try to reach you. I'm assuming he was unsuccessful."

Lacey felt her cheeks heat and struggled to keep her composure.

"I'm very sorry to disappoint you, Ms. Duggan."

Lacey blinked and got herself together. She called up a smile. "Me, too, but perhaps you can keep my résumé on file? In case anything else comes up in your accounting department in the future."

Ms. Blackwood's face lightened. "I certainly will. Can we offer you a coffee or something?"

"I'm fine," she answered, trying to mask her disappointment. "But maybe I'll leave you my cell number as well as my home number."

Ms. Blackwood seemed to appreciate the wry sense of humor and nodded. "Give it to Jane, here, and she'll put it on your résumé. It was nice to meet you."

They shook hands again, and then Lacey found herself back outside the office door.

She walked across the parking lot, the winter air freezing against her legs. Stupid shoes...she'd worn them for vanity and now it was for nothing and she was freezing her toes off. She turned on the car and finally looked at her phone. There were two text messages, one from Quinn and one from Duke.

The first one said Call home as soon as you get this. Q.

The second was the one that Duke had sent while she was in the office. Did Quinn get in touch with you?

She texted Duke back right away and let him know she was on her way back. Then she texted Quinn and simply replied that she'd just received his text and thanks.

Quinn already knew, then, that she didn't get the job. Great. She loved looking like a failure in front of him.

Worse, his truck was still in the yard when she got home. She would have preferred to lick her wounds in peace, but apparently today was just not her lucky day. Wearily she turned the key in the door and walked in, only to hear the television going and some very girlish laughter.

Amber was here.

Lacey tried to be annoyed but she couldn't. Amber was a total doll, clearly more like her mother than her father. She smiled easily and had gorgeous curls that set off a pair of impish blue eyes. Lacey shut the door and put her handbag on the first step of the stairs, then slipped off her heels. The office door to her right was closed; Quinn was probably in there working. She went through on stocking feet and found Amber sitting at the table, coloring some sheets that Lacey guessed were from school, and watching cartoons.

"Well, hello," she greeted. "Whatcha got there?"

"Lacey! Daddy said you were here!"

To her surprise, Amber hopped down from the chair and hugged Lacey's legs.

Suddenly the day didn't seem so gray.

"Okay, okay. No day care today?"

"Miss Melanie was sick today. Daddy came to pick me up after school, but he said he had some work to do first so I could watch TV." She looked up at Lacey, her eyes troubled. "Is that okay? You live here. Maybe Daddy should have asked p'mission."

God, if the kid were any more sweet she'd be made of sugar. "It's perfectly fine. You go ahead and carry on with the coloring. I'm going to change out of my clothes, okay?"

"But why? You look pretty."

Now there was a compliment that was heartfelt and Lacey smiled a little. "Why, thank you. But I think I'll put on something a little more comfortable so I can cook some dinner."

Instead of getting back in her seat, Amber followed Lacey down the hall to the stairs. "What are you going to make?" she asked, and Lacey hid a smile.

"If you were me, what would you make for supper?"

Amber followed her up the stairs. "I would make… fried chicken and 'tato salad."

It sounded like a strange order, and Lacey looked down at her companion. "Really?"

Amber nodded. "'Cause it's Daddy's favorite only he doesn't know how to make it and I'm too little."

And just like that Lacey's heart did a little turn. Quinn and Amber did the best they could. It wasn't hard to forgive him for his earlier sharpness. After all, he'd tried to pass on the message right away and it was her own fault she hadn't gotten the text. That she'd gotten lost.

"Now, what a coincidence! I was just going to make that!"

Amber turned her head sideways and peered up at Lacey as they reached the top step. "What's a coinc'dence?" She struggled over the word.

Lacey smiled. "Well, it's like taking two things that aren't related at all and connecting them together."

"Like me and my best friend, Emma? We're not related but purple is both our favorite color."

Bad grammar and all, Lacey was enchanted. "Well, sort of like that."

Amber actually followed her right into the bedroom and plopped up on the bed while Lacey went to the closet for a pair of sweats and an old hoodie. Not sure how Quinn would feel about Amber's intrusion, she did a quick change right in the closet and came out in her comfy clothes.

"Ta-da! Presto chango!"

Amber fell over on the bed in a fit of giggles.

"Amber? Where'd you go?"

"Uh-oh," the girl whispered, crawling off the bed. She stuck her head out the bedroom door. "I'm up here, Daddy."

"You're not supposed to wander around upstairs. You know that."

Lacey was right behind her. "That's okay. She came up with me."

Quinn's face changed, adopting that impersonal mask again that Lacey was starting to hate. "Oh. I didn't know you were back." He looked at Amber again. "Don't you go bothering Lacey, now."

"Sorry, Daddy."

Lacey put her hand on Amber's curls. "It's okay. I had a cruddy afternoon and Amber's a real ray of sunshine."

"You're sure?"

Lacey nodded. "I'm sure. Tell you what." She squatted down beside Amber. "Sometimes when you come over, I might not have time to hang out. If I tell you that I'm busy, you'll respect that, right?"

Amber's little head bobbed up and down. "I won't get in your way."

Lacey got the feeling that Amber's life revolved a little too much around being out of the way. Her heart ached for the little girl. Lacey wasn't a stranger to that sensation, either. Being the middle child in a single-parent home, she'd often felt invisible. Superfluous.

She held out her hand and they went down the stairs together, with Quinn waiting at the bottom. She could tell by the set of his jaw that he was tense about it. "Amber, why don't you go tidy up your crayons? Then you can help me in the kitchen if you want."

"Yay!" Amber raced off, while Lacey faced Quinn at the bottom of the stairs.

"You don't have to babysit her," he said quietly, so his daughter couldn't hear. "She's used to amusing herself while I finish up."

It hurt a little to say, but she did it anyway. "Quinn, I like kids. Amber's sweet. I mean it. If she's in my way, I'll speak up. But you know I had a rotten afternoon. She really did perk it up."

"You didn't get my text, did you?"

She shook her head. "Not until after I'd gotten lost, ripped my panty hose, spilled water down my front and was told the position was already filled."

He laughed then, a dry chuckle that made her smile. "I know. It sounds ridiculous," she added.

"I'm sorry," he offered, and this time she knew he meant it.

"Ah well, it was my first nibble and it's only been a few days. Something will turn up."

"Yes, it will." His gaze was warmer as he looked at her and there was a moment where she got the feeling they almost…understood each other. But that was nuts. Oil and water. That's what they were…what she had to remember.

And she remembered the way he'd told her she looked pretty and got a little whoop-y feeling in her stomach.

"I'd better finish up," he said softly, and for the briefest moment his gaze dropped to her lips. Oh. Oh, my. She sucked in a breath.

"Okay."

Quinn left her standing there, still reeling from the split second where he'd stared at her mouth. He couldn't be attracted to her. Couldn't have thought about kissing her. He didn't even like her!

She didn't like him, either, but if she were honest, the thought had crossed her mind that kissing him might not be so bad.

The door to the office closed and she shook her head. Fried chicken. Potato salad. She'd better get on it if they planned to have a decent dinner.

AMBER WAS AS much a distraction as a help in the kitchen, but Lacey didn't mind. She cut up the potatoes and Amber put them in the pot, and then while they waited for them to cook, Lacey set the girl to work mixing dressing for the salad while she put together seasoning for the chicken. Together they decided on frozen corn for a side, with a dish of sliced cucumbers, Amber's favorite raw vegetable. Potatoes were drained and rinsed repeatedly in cold water to cool them down, and Lacey started frying the chicken while Amber poured corn kernels in a casserole dish for heating in the microwave. They agreed on celery and a little red pepper in the salad but no onion, and by the time Quinn came out of his office, the chicken was frying merrily in a pan, the salad was in a pretty scalloped bowl, and the microwave was running.

"What on earth is all this?" he asked, staring at the mess on the countertops.

"We made dinner! I helped! It's your favorite, Daddy. Fried chicken!"

She looked up at him so happily that Lacey could tell he didn't have the heart to scowl.

"Fried chicken? How did you know that's my favorite?"

"Chicken and 'tato salad! Everyone knows that." She rolled her eyes and Lacey laughed.

"You're expected to stay, you know." She said it softly, holding a pair of tongs in her hand. "I made enough for all of us. This way you don't have to go home and worry about supper."

She could tell that Quinn was torn. After their conversation at noon, this was exactly what he said he didn't want. She lifted her chin. "It was Amber's idea," she added.

His gaze held hers. Momentarily she felt guilty for putting his little girl in the middle, but Amber was very hard to resist. Couldn't he see how happy his daughter looked right now?

"Amber, why don't you set the table? Do you know where everything is?" she asked, breaking the connection.

Amber nodded and raced for a step stool that allowed her to reach the plates and glasses in the cupboard. Lacey turned the chicken in the pan, putting the splatter screen over the top again to keep the grease from dotting the top of the stove. She heard Quinn behind her, helping Amber put things on the table in preparation for the meal.

It felt homey. It felt…like everything Lacey was sure she'd been missing. Only this wasn't her family. Not her husband, not her daughter, not her home. It was just pretend. Something to make her feel better, to fill the gap until she got her life in order again.

And if now and again it gave Quinn a hand, all the better.

When had she started caring?

The chicken was perfectly done and she removed it from the pan and put it on a platter. The salad was placed in the middle of the table, and she added a sprinkle of paprika for color, then put the bowl of corn on a hot mat and stirred in just a little bit of butter. "There," she said, stepping back. "All done. Let's eat."

She took the spot at the foot of the table while Quinn sat at the head, where he normally ate his lunch, and Amber was in between them on the side. Lacey watched as Quinn helped Amber put salad, corn and cucumbers on her plate, and then chose a drumstick for her to eat. Her eyes were huge as she looked at all the food and then, just as Lacey was about to taste her first bite of potato salad, Amber dropped her fork with a clatter.

"Daddy! We forgot to say grace!"

He put down his fork. "So we did."

Amber turned her face to Lacey. "Do you want to say it, Lacey?"

Lacey struggled to answer. Grace was not really her thing. They'd never said it at home at mealtime and she wasn't quite comfortable right now, being put on the spot.

"Why don't you say it, sweetie?" Quinn came to the rescue and made the suggestion.

"Okay." When Lacey sat still, Amber held out her hand. "We hold hands, like this," she said, wiggling her fingers.

Hesitantly Lacey took the little fingers in her own, and watched as Quinn held Amber's other hand. Her heart melted a little bit as Amber's eyes squinted shut.

Lacey was expecting a scripted blessing, sort of the "God is great, God is good" thing she remembered from vacation Bible school when she'd spent time here at Crooked Valley when she was little. But instead, Amber took a few seconds to think before she offered up a simple prayer.

"Dear God, thank you for fried chicken and 'tato salad and for my daddy and for my friend Lacey. Amen."

When she was done she dropped their hands, picked up her drumstick and took a bite, utterly unconcerned.

But Lacey met Quinn's gaze and saw something there she wasn't prepared for. She saw beyond the ranch manager and her biggest critic and the single dad to the man beneath.

And that man made her catch her breath.

Chapter Four

January turned into February. Lacey had two more interviews and no callbacks, which was highly discouraging.
After the dinner at the ranch, she hadn't seen Amber.
Miss Melanie was feeling better and Amber went back to
day care after school each day. Quinn made an obvious
effort to stay out of Lacey's way, too—eating his lunch
in the office, or taking it out to the barn and eating with
the hands around the coffee break table.

Lacey got the message loud and clear. If Quinn had
been feeling any attraction, he certainly didn't want to
act on it.

She occasionally sent home dinner with him. Some
sliced baked ham and scalloped potatoes, or a dish of
chili, or a casserole of lasagna for him to share with
Amber. Quinn always protested, and she always answered the same way: she wasn't going to eat badly
just because she was cooking for one. He might as well
take the extra because she was going to cook it anyway.

The fact that he reluctantly agreed told her that he
was glad to have the help even if he wouldn't admit it.

One sunshine-y day she printed out a few ads and
drove into Gibson, hoping to put them up at the super-
market and post office and anywhere else she might find

a bulletin board. Truth was, her unemployment checks were covering her expenses so far, but her real problem was having too much time on her hands. She needed something to keep her busy or she was going to eat too many brownies and fancy breads and end up requiring a whole new wardrobe. Taking on odd accounting jobs wasn't ideal but it was better than nothing. The businesses in Gibson were small, independently owned ones rather than big chains. Surely someone would be in need of some bookkeeping help.

She pinned up her notice on the community board at the grocery store, the drugstore, at the post office and at the office that housed the Chamber of Commerce. Then she ventured across the street to the library in the hopes of posting one there, which she left with the librarian. At the diner, she grabbed some lunch at the counter and asked if she could leave one there. Before going home, she stopped at the town's one and only department store, looking for some new dishcloths and some replacement pairs of panty hose just in case she got any more interview calls. She stopped in front of a Valentine's Day display and smiled a little at the boxes of kids' cards generally featuring characters from the latest animated movies or TV shows. She picked up one set that was from Amber's favorite cartoon. Amber would probably have her first school party this year and give cards to all her classmates. On a whim, Lacey put the box in her basket and also snagged a few paper decorations and craft kits.

She was just adding a small bag of foil-wrapped chocolate hearts when she ran into Kailey Brandt, wheeling a cart full of towels that were on sale, cleaning supplies and a box of file folders.

"Lacey! Hey there." Kailey stopped the cart and smiled at Lacey, though Lacey thought she could see some strain around the other woman's eyes. "What brings you into town?"

"Oh, this and that," she replied, suddenly feeling rather awkward that she was still out of work.

"Paper Valentines?" Kailey grinned. "Amber's been around some, huh?"

"Not much. But I saw them and I couldn't resist. It's been a long time since I handed out Valentine's Day cards."

Kailey nodded. "If you were like the rest of us around here, you decorated shoeboxes for a mailbox and ate way too many heart-shaped cookies at the class party."

They both laughed a little. "Those were the days, right? Far less complicated."

"Tell me about it," Kailey said, her shoulders slumping. "I'm trying to keep the tax stuff straight and I ran out of file folders. I swear to God, I can work with ornery horses all day long, but doing paperwork is like the seventh circle of hell."

Lacey's ears definitely perked up at that, but it seemed presumptuous to offer her services during a friendly, neighborly exchange at the department store. She paused and then cautiously asked, "Have you considered outsourcing it?"

Kailey nodded. "A few times. I only took over a few years ago after my mom got thrown and hit her head. She does okay most of the time, but she struggles with numbers now and deals with migraines a lot."

"I didn't know. Your poor mom."

Kailey smiled. "She manages, and she just does other stuff. But she's slowed down a lot and Dad doesn't have the patience for accounting. That leaves me, unless I hire an accountant. The office in town is pretty expensive and I'd have to take the stuff there, you know? It's more trouble than it's worth, so I suffer. Usually not in silence." She laughed at herself a little.

It would be the perfect situation. "You know I'm an accountant, right?" she asked.

"Yeah, but I figured you'd be looking for something full-time. We don't have a huge operation, Lacey. It's just a few hours here and there, with a little more at tax time."

Lacey shrugged. "So? If I can do a few hours for you, and find some other businesses with the same needs…it would at least get me out of the house and doing something other than going crazy."

"I can't imagine wanting to do math rather than be in a barn," Kailey said. "Let me talk it over with my dad. How much would you charge?"

Lacey named her hourly rate—a little on the low side, taking into consideration that budgets were probably a little tight in a small ranching community.

"You're staying at the house? I'll give you a call. Because honestly, you'd be doing me a huge favor if I didn't have to worry about this stuff."

"Yep. If I don't answer, just leave a message and I'll get back to you." For the first time in weeks she felt a sliver of hope. Even if she ended up getting a position somewhere on a more permanent basis, she could manage a single client after hours.

At that moment Kailey's cell phone rang and she frowned. "Weird. Hardly anyone ever calls me. Most of the time they text." She dug around in her purse and found the phone. "It's Carrie. I hope there's nothing wrong." She answered it at the same time as Lacey's phone began to ring.

A strange feeling crawled through Lacey's stomach. She looked at her phone and saw Duke's number on the display. She swallowed as she hit the accept button. She hoped it was nothing with the baby. That would be terrible for them and a little too close to home for her.

"Duke? What's wrong?"

"Thank God I got you. Where are you?"

"In town, shopping."

"Can you stop by the preschool and pick up Amber rather than her going to day care?"

The crawly feeling intensified. "What's happened? Is Quinn all right?"

"He'll be fine. There was a fire at his place, though. He tried to stop it while he was waiting for the fire department."

Gibson was so small that the department was volunteer-based. Response time could be slow...

"Is he hurt? What about the house?" Dread spiraled through her. Please let him be okay, she thought. And poor Amber. She didn't need any more upheaval, either...

"The house will be fine, eventually. Quinn kept it confined to the kitchen area and the department got there in time to knock it down. It'll need gutting, though. And Quinn...he got a few burns. He's on his way to the hospital now."

She lowered her voice. "How bad, Duke?"

"Not that bad," he assured her. "But he needs proper treatment and the burns are going to be tender for a while."

She closed her eyes, thinking of Quinn in pain, picturing him trying to fight the fire all on his own. Stupid, brave man.

"I'll get Amber. Should I come to the hospital?"

"No." Duke's voice was firm. "I don't know how much she remembers from when Marie died, but there's no need to freak her out. Just take her back to the house after school. I think she's done at noon."

Lacey caught Kailey's worried gaze and knew they were getting the same information.

"Don't worry about it, Duke. I'll take care of it."

"Thanks. We're going to head in to the hospital now."

"Then come to supper at the house. I'll cook for everyone. Amber can help and it'll be good to keep her busy. She likes helping in the kitchen."

"You're a gem, Lace."

Gem, huh? Truth was, she was more worried than she cared to admit about Quinn and she would benefit from being occupied. "Don't worry about it. Just text me with updates, okay?"

"Can do."

She hung up at the same time as Kailey and they looked at each other. Lacey wondered if her face looked as worried as Kailey's.

"You heard the news," Kailey said quietly.

"Yeah. Duke asked if I'd pick Amber up after school. I hope he's right, that Quinn's burns are minor."

"Me, too. Gosh, that family has been through enough."

Lacey remembered what it was like to lose a parent at a young age. And she remembered how frightening it was to think that something might happen to the one left behind. "This might be the perfect day for some Valentine's Day planning," Lacey said tightly.

"I've got to head home for a bit, but I offered to help the guys with the chores tonight. That way Duke and Carrie can look after Quinn."

Lacey had nearly forgotten what it was like to live in

a small town, but the current crisis reminded her. "Listen, I'm going to cook for everyone. You're welcome to stay too, if you don't have to rush back home."

"Thanks." Kailey tucked her phone back in her purse. "I'll play it by ear, see when things get finished." She reached out and squeezed Lacey's arm. "Give Amber my love, okay? She's a sweetie."

"I will. See you back at the ranch."

Kailey rushed off to pay for her items and Lacey checked her watch. She still had some time before she needed to pick Amber up from school, so she added a few more craft supplies to the cart, and then threw in what she guessed to be the right size pajamas and set of yoga pants with a matching shirt, just in case Amber needed a change of clothes. Once she'd paid for those, she headed to the grocery store and picked up whatever was missing from the pantry for tonight's supper. There would be at least five of them to eat, six if Kailey was there, so she picked up a large roast and an extra bag of carrots. Fresh green beans were on sale, and she bought whipping cream and a bag of apples. On the way out, she snagged a couple of bottles of red wine. Once her groceries were stowed in the trunk along with her other purchases, she found it was nearly dismissal time and made her way to the school.

It worked out perfectly. She got there just ahead of the lunch bell. She explained the situation, and the young woman behind the desk said that Carrie had already called—she was on file as the emergency contact for Quinn. It wasn't until Amber had been paged to come to the office that Lacey realized she had no idea what to say to the little girl. She didn't want to be the one to tell her that there'd been a fire in her house. Quinn should be the one to do that. Amber was skipping down the hall towards the office. Lacey had to think of something fast.

"Lacey!" Amber came right up and gave her a hug. "Just a minute. I need to see Miss J."

Politely Amber went to the young woman's desk. "Hi, Miss J."

The secretary smiled at Amber. "Miss Duggan is here to take you home today, Amber."

"I'm not going to day care?"

"Not today."

Amber looked over at Lacey. "But only Daddy or Carrie is supposed to pick me up from school."

Lacey went to a chair and sat down so she was more on Amber's level. "Carrie already called the office and said it would be okay."

"What about Daddy?" Amber's little face wrinkled with confusion. She was so delightfully innocent.

"Well, your daddy had to go into town for a while. But I went shopping this morning and I have a surprise in the car for you. We're going to spend the afternoon together."

"We are? Yay! I have to go to my classroom and get my stuff."

She turned around and gave Miss J a wave. "Bye, Miss J!"

While Lacey waited, the secretary got a binder from behind the desk and put it up front for Lacey to sign. "It's a sign-out log," she said. "I hope Quinn's all right."

"Duke said he'll be fine. I'm not sure what to tell Amber, though, so I'm going to hold off for a bit. We're going to make Valentines today and do some cooking."

Amber was back just as the lunch bell rang. "Okay Lacey, let's go!" she declared, her curls bouncing.

Once at home, Amber helped carry in the bags, chattering the whole time. "Did you bring my lunch?" she asked. "Daddy left it on the counter this morning. He said he'd go get it and bring it to me but he never did. He musta forgotted."

Lacey halted, her hand inside a grocery bag. Was that why Quinn had been home when the fire started? What might have happened if he hadn't been there? What if they'd lost everything?

"Lacey? You look funny."

She pasted on a smile. "Just thinking. I don't have your lunch, so let's make something. What's your favorite?"

"Grilled cheese!" Amber jumped up and down while Lacey wondered where she got all her energy. "With pickles!"

"Grilled cheese it is." She got Amber set up at the stove, standing on a step stool, armed with a spatula while the sandwiches fried, and Lacey put the groceries away, keeping a keen eye on her little chef. Amber did great, though, and Lacey cut up little dill pickles to go with their sandwiches and before long they were at the table munching. Once the mess was tidied, Lacey got out the Valentine's Day supplies which sent Amber into fits of rapture. Lacey found a shoebox upstairs in a closet and together they cut a mail slot in the lid and covered it with aluminum foil to make it shiny. After that Amber decorated the outside with red and pink and white foam hearts and stickers that had messages like "Happy Valentine's Day" and "Be Mine" on them. All in all, Amber was delighted with the result, but when it came to cleaning up the mess she lacked her usual enthusiasm.

Once the table was cleared of the paper and foil scraps, Lacey put on a few cartoons and Amber went to chill on the sofa. Five minutes later she was asleep.

Lacey checked her phone. Still no text from Duke.

She worked around the kitchen as quietly as she could, searing the roast and then putting it in the oven, peeling carrots and stemming the beans. Both were in pots on the stove when she started peeling potatoes, and her phone buzzed on the counter.

Her hands were damp so she dried them on a towel and reached for the phone. It was a text message, and her heart gave a little skip when she saw that it was from Quinn and not Duke.

How's Amber?

She typed back quickly. Fine. Asleep on the sofa. Are you okay?

Nothing serious. A few bandages. We should be out of here soon.

She didn't even get the reply typed when the next message came.

What did you tell her?

Lacey backspaced out what she'd been typing and simply responded, Nothing. Thought she needed to hear it from her daddy.

A pause. Then another buzz.

Thank you, Lace.

Why a simple thank-you made her eyes sting she had no idea. You're sure you're okay? she asked.

You worried about me? And then a winky face. Lacey
frowned, feeling disturbingly transparent.

Amber woke from her nap, and Lacey typed back
quickly. Amber's awake. Going to make dessert. Don't
be late for supper. Huh. He needed to know that nothing had changed where they were concerned. She wasn't
going to get all mushy and weird or let him off easily.

Except she was. She just wasn't going to give him the
satisfaction of knowing it. Who knew what he'd do with
that sort of information in his pocket?

LACEY HAD TEXTED CARRIE, requesting that Carrie let her
know when they were about a half hour away. When the
text came, Lacey and Amber were just taking the apple
upside-down cake out of the oven. After that, Lacey
turned on the vegetables while Amber set the table. By
the time the entourage arrived, she'd put the roast to rest
and was whisking red wine into the drippings in preparation for thickening it for gravy.

"Daddy Daddy Daddy!" Before Lacey could inter-
vene, Amber went rushing to the door. There was a beat
of silence, then Amber's shaky voice. "What happened
to your hand, Daddy?"

Duke and Carrie appeared in the kitchen, their faces
tired and drawn. "I don't envy him that conversation,"
Carrie said quietly.

She no sooner had it out of her mouth than Amber
started crying. The pitiful sound filtered down the hall
and into the kitchen where Lacey was stirring the gravy
as if her life depended on it. Hearing Amber cry put a
lump in her throat and tears in her eyes. Then the low
tones of Quinn's response hit her square in the gut. How
many times had he broken bad news to his little girl?

of water and handed it to him. "It hurts a lot, huh?" she asked in an undertone.

"Like the devil," he replied, wincing.

"I'm so sorry, Quinn." Before she moved away she put her hand on his shoulder and squeezed. Her fingers were sliding away when he reached up and grabbed her hand.

"Thank you. For all you did today. I can never repay you."

"No worries." She pulled her hand away, not wanting him to know how much the simple touch affected her.

"I mean it, Lacey. We had a few moments of upset, but she's taking it well. She feels safe here. Safe with you."

"I'm glad," she responded. "I know how important she is to you, Quinn. She's a great kid and you're a fine father."

It didn't even hurt to say, except perhaps in a bitter-sweet way. Her heart went out to both of them. The way anyone's would, she reasoned with herself.

Too bad she didn't quite believe it.

Chapter Five

Kailey went home and Carrie and Lacey tackled the dishes while Quinn and Duke got down to business.

"You'll stay here," Duke announced. "You can't go home until everything's been fixed up right. We'll contact the insurance company first thing in the morning. Hopefully it won't take too long. In the meantime, you and Amber are welcome to stay here. Right, Lacey?"

She didn't know why she hadn't thought of this. She'd assumed maybe they'd spend the night here tonight; it was why she'd bought Amber the pajamas after all. But move in? They'd be...roommates.

When she didn't answer, the silence grew awkward. "Hey," Quinn said into the quiet, "don't worry about it. I have options."

"What options?" Duke persisted.

"It's fine," Lacey agreed, even though she was far from comfortable with the idea. Having the 8:00 a.m. to 6:00 p.m. rule was one thing. Having Quinn here 24/7 was quite another. She liked her privacy. Liked her freedom. She really wasn't in the market for a roommate. Plus, she was trying to say the right thing in the middle of being blindsided.

Except Quinn had just temporarily lost his home.

This was Duke's place and he'd offered it to Lacey when she needed it. Why shouldn't he offer it to his manager and friend in his time of need as well?

"The Rogers kid is right on this road," Duke insisted. "I bet Amber can catch a ride with them in the mornings and still go to day care in the afternoons. Come on, man." He lowered his voice. "You know she's comfortable here. It would be less of an adjustment for her, you know?"

Lacey nodded, even though she had misgivings. "It's true, Quinn. There's lots of room here. And it's about what's best for Amber."

Maybe he wouldn't need this place for long. Or maybe one of her interviews would work out and she would be able to get out and get her own place.

"I hate imposing."

"It's not imposing," Carrie insisted. "If anyone else were in this situation, you'd do what you could to help and you know it."

"I don't even have anything for tonight." He sighed heavily. "I never even thought. All of Amber's stuff is at the house. And it is all probably smoke-damaged." He closed his eyes wearily.

"I've got spare toothbrushes at the bunkhouse. I'll bring them up," Carrie offered. "And you're close to the same size as Duke. I'll get you a change of clothes, and you can throw those ones in the washer."

"I bought Amber some stuff on impulse today," Lacey admitted. "Just in case she needed emergency clothes. I hope I got the right size. There are pajamas for tonight and an outfit for tomorrow. When she changes for bed, I'll wash up her clothes, too. I'll just throw some of mine in with them."

Quinn looked as if he'd aged ten years. "I don't know what to say. Thank you all. So much."

"As Carrie said, you'd do the same for any of us." Duke put his hand on Quinn's shoulder. "I'll go grab you a change of clothes."

"And I'll send up some toiletries. We'll worry about the rest tomorrow," Carrie said.

When they were gone, that just left Quinn and Lacey, and a tired-out Amber sprawled on the sofa with a book from her backpack.

Quinn sighed, got up from the table, went into the living room and sat beside her.

"So." He patted her leg. "I'm afraid we can't go home tonight, sweetheart."

Amber looked up. "But it's my bedtime soon."

Quinn swallowed several times and Lacey understood. The day was catching up to him and he was struggling to hold it together.

"What your dad means is that everyone is really tired and we were wondering if you'd like to have a sleepover here tonight." Lacey went closer and knelt by the sofa.

"On a school night?" The way she said it made it sound like the worst, most wonderful transgression.

"Yes, on a school night. I even picked out a pair of jammies for you at the store today. If you want, you can have a bath in my tub and use my bubble bath."

"Really?"

"Yes, really."

Suddenly Amber frowned. "But I don't gots any underwear."

Quinn jumped into the conversation again. "What about the secret emergency pair in the pocket of your backpack?"

Amber's eyes lit up. "Oh, yeah!"

"So what do you think? Should we run you a bath?"

Amber nodded so quickly her ponytail bobbed up and down. "Bubbles! I love bubbles!"

She was off like a shot, running up the stairs and into the bathroom. Lacey treated Quinn to a sideways grin. "Did we ever have that much energy as kids?"

"We must have, though I don't remember."

He closed his eyes and she realized he must be exhausted. "You rest for a bit. I'll look after Amber."

"You're sure?"

"Positive."

He didn't even argue. Just let out a long sigh and kept his eyes closed. And that was what really worried Lacey. No smart remark, no protest…he was just letting her call the shots. It was so not like him that she guessed he was hurting more than he let on.

Amber loved the bubbles and after she'd washed her hair with Lacey's shampoo, Lacey wrapped her in an oversize towel and reached for the pajamas. They were light purple with pink and blue and yellow butterflies all over them and Amber was delighted, her chatter still going as she stepped into clean underwear and the bottoms. There was a brief reprieve as they pulled the top over her head but then she was off again, babbling about how tomorrow they'd have to go get her things from the house and get her teddy bears and toys. Lacey just let her go, because she didn't want to make any promises she might not be able to keep. She had no idea what sort of state the house was in.

Once the bath was over, though, it seemed Amber's insecurities returned. Carrie and Duke popped in briefly with the promised items but disappeared again. When

Quinn announced it was time for Amber to go to bed, her eyes grew troubled and her face fell. "But Daddy, I don't want to go to bed yet."

"You need your rest for school tomorrow, pumpkin."

"But I want to go get my clothes and toys tomorrow."

Quinn's face tightened. "Honey, I'm not sure how that's going to work yet."

Tears swam in her eyes. "But I want my stuff! I can't sleep without Mary!"

Quinn sighed. "It's just a teddy bear, Amber."

"She's not! She's my favorite bear! I sleep with her every night!"

A teddy bear named Mary. Was it a coincidence that Amber's mom's name had been Marie? If Lacey's heart was aching right now, what must Quinn be going through?

"Would you like to borrow my teddy bear?" Lacey asked, heat blooming in her cheeks. She avoided looking at Quinn. A grown woman with a stuffed animal. She suspected he'd have some choice words about that.

"You have a bear?"

Lacey nodded. She wasn't even sure why she kept the damn thing. It was too hard to let go completely, she supposed. The soft brown bear with the red ribbon was something Carter had bought her when they'd first decided to try having a baby. They'd planned on giving it to their son or daughter as a first stuffed animal. As the months went on, she'd put the bear in the back of the closet. When everything had fallen apart, she probably should have gotten rid of it, but she somehow couldn't stand the thought of letting it go.

Amber might as well have it. At least it would be

loved and not…well, not reminding Lacey of something that would never come to pass.

"I do. And you're welcome to have it."

Amber considered for a moment, and then went over to Quinn and crawled up beside him. "Daddy? Do you think Mary will be okay at home alone? I mean, won't she be scared sleeping all by herself?"

The tension eased in Quinn's face. "Honey, you know Mary has all sorts of stuffed animal friends keeping her company on your bed. She'll be fine."

"It's scary sleeping alone, Daddy."

Lacey saw him swallow. "Would you like to bunk with me tonight?"

The still-damp curls bobbed as she nodded. "Uh-huh."

"Let's go tuck you in, then. I promise I'll be up later."

"Promise?"

"Absolutely."

Lacey retrieved the bear and got an extra blanket for the spare bedroom. The bed was a queen, so there would be lots of room for both Quinn and Amber. There was no night-light, though, so Lacey left the light on in the bathroom so the upstairs wasn't pitch-black. Quinn came upstairs and once Amber brushed her teeth they tucked her in and Lacey tucked the bear in with her. It felt right, passing it on. Like something she should have done ages ago. On impulse she leaned down and kissed Amber's forehead. "Good night, sweetie."

"Night, Lacey."

"Go to sleep, baby." Quinn kissed her, too. "I'll be up soon."

"Okay, Daddy."

They left the door open, and made their way back

downstairs. Quinn went back to the living room and sank into the soft cushions of the sofa, letting out a breath.

Lacey went straight to the cupboard above the stove and took out a bottle of whiskey that she assumed had once been her grandfather's before he died. She poured a healthy splash in two glasses and went back to the living room, handed Quinn a glass, and sat across from him on the love seat.

"Hell of a day," she said quietly, and Quinn nodded.

"Yep." He took a long drink of his whiskey and winced as he swallowed. "Gah."

Lacey did the same, felt the burn of the liquor heat her belly. "Are you sure you're okay?"

"This?" He lifted one bandaged arm. "It'll heal. I wish other things could be fixed as easily."

"Do you mean the house or your daughter?"

He drained the rest of the whiskey. "Both. Amber's had such a rough time. Our home was the one thing I could do to keep things consistent for her, you know? So she could see that not everything changed after Marie…" He paused and cleared his throat. "After she died. Now that's changed, too. I didn't want to tell her but there's a lot of smoke damage. Most of our things are ruined. A crew is going to have to go in there and do a major cleanup and the kitchen and downstairs bath will have to be rebuilt. Even then, those are just things. I hate that she's feeling so insecure again. That there's nothing I can do to keep her world the same as it was before."

"Except that you're still here and with her every step of the way."

"A kid her age doesn't get that. They see a change in routine, in familiar things, and fear. Tell me a fire wouldn't have scared the living shit out of you when you were four years old."

"I was six when a man in a uniform knocked on the door and told me my father was dead, Quinn. My mom moved us to the city. New people, new place, new everything. I know what you mean, but I also know that it meant the world to me to have my mom. Duke and Rylan were boys. They had each other. I was alone in the middle. I understand more than you think."

There was silence for a minute, and then Quinn reluctantly admitted, "I know you do. I'm sorry."

Lacey shook her head. "Don't be sorry at all. I'm not saying you're wrong. I'm just saying…" She searched for the right words. "Amber is lucky to have you, and even at her age, she knows it."

"She was afraid I was going to die like her mother. That damn near broke my heart."

"Of course it did. There's nothing worse than knowing your child is in pain."

Quinn winced as he shifted in the chair. "What would you know about it?"

Well, damn. Just when she let her guard down, thought she and Quinn were working together, bam. He knew exactly where to hit her so it hurt the most.

She finished her drink. Considered explaining and then decided against it. It was her private business, for one, and today wasn't about her. Quinn had a lot on his plate and she wasn't about to bring her drama into it. Another day she might have pointed out all she'd done to help and perhaps he could show a little gratitude. But not today. Not with something this big.

So she bit her tongue and instead asked about the house. "Do they have any idea what caused the fire?"

Quinn met her gaze. "Do you think Amber's asleep?"

It was an odd question, and she frowned at him. "Why?"

His voice was low as he answered. "I don't want her to hear."

It had been several minutes and the house was utterly silent. "She was exhausted. I'm sure she's asleep."

Quinn nodded. "Before school she came out with lipstick on and I sent her back to the bathroom to wipe it off. She must have gotten into some of Marie's things without me knowing. What I didn't realize was that she'd gotten out the straightening iron. The initial guess is that we left before she could use it and it got left on, since the fire seems to have started in the half bath. I can't think of anything else that would have done it." He scrubbed his face with a hand. "She misses her mom so much. Even now, after all this time. I know that. I should have checked before we left the house, but we were running late."

"You couldn't have known. Don't blame yourself."

His face hardened. "I'm sure as hell not going to blame her, if that's what you're getting at."

The whiskey hadn't done anything to ease his mood, and Lacey thought perhaps bed was a better idea. "I wasn't blaming anyone, and neither should you. That's why it's called an accident."

She pushed herself off the love seat and went to the kitchen, put her glass in the sink. "It's been a long day. I think I'll say good-night," she said, and headed for the stairs.

Quinn got up and followed her. "Lacey, wait."

She shouldn't have paused. She should have kept right on going, around the newel post and up the stairs to her room and shut the door. But she didn't. Her footsteps halted and he caught up with her. His fingers circled her forearm, turning her around to face him.

"I'm sorry I snapped at you," he said, his voice deep and low. "That was uncalled for."

She swallowed, unsure of what to say. "It's okay," she whispered, anxious to get away, terrified by how much she liked the feel of his hand on her wrist. Her breath came quick and shallow and when she looked up and their eyes met…

Let me go, she thought crazily. *Let me go because we can't do this.*

"It's not okay," he answered, and his hand tightened until she was sure he had to feel her pulse hammering against his fingertips. "You've done nothing but help today. You even thought to pick up things for my daughter just in case, and you cooked for all of us, and I know you must hate having us intrude on your space…"

"It's fine—"

"…and the first chance I get, I'm snapping at you."

"It's been a challenging day."

"And now you're making excuses for me. When what I should be doing is saying thank-you."

She was certain her heart was going to beat clear through her chest when he pulled her closer and folded her in a hug. "Thank you," he whispered. "For taking care of my daughter as if she were your own."

Her eyes stung. His first words had been like a stab to the gut. But this…this was taking the knife and twisting it.

It was all she could do to not start crying.

"I don't know what we would have done without you today. She was so scared…hell, I was terrified. I walked in there and smelled the smoke and saw the flames and all I could think of was stopping it so we didn't lose what we had left of our old life."

He held her closer and she let him, because she could tell he needed to say it, to get it out in the open. It wasn't just Amber who'd been traumatized today. Quinn had been, too. His word choice said a lot, too. He was holding tight to the life they used to have. It wasn't the first time he'd said it. It was the life he'd had with Marie, when they'd all been a happy family. She had no business inserting herself into the middle of that.

Inserting herself? That was crazy, wasn't it? She didn't even like Quinn…

Except deep down she knew that was a lie. Yes, he got under her skin. Yes, she often felt inadequate when he was around. There wasn't anything he did poorly. But she did like him, or at least admire him. Too much for her own good. Too much for them to be living under the same roof and definitely too much for her to spend any longer in his embrace.

She gave a quick squeeze and then started to pull away. "But you are here, and everything is going to be fine. Just remember that." She stepped out of his embrace and smiled weakly. "Before you know it everything will be back to normal and this will all be behind you."

His gaze searched hers and she wondered if the whiskey had been extra strong.

"Back to normal. Right."

"I'm going to bed, Quinn. It's been a long day."

"Right."

"See you in the morning."

"Right again."

And still his gaze held her prisoner until she either had to break it or she was going to find herself in his arms again.

It was the reminder of Marie that made her back up a little more. His hand rested on the railing of the staircase and the plain gold band on his finger caught the light. It communicated their situation perfectly: Quinn Solomon was still another woman's husband. In his heart, where it mattered most. In that moment she was incredibly jealous of Marie Solomon. How lucky the woman had been, to know that much love and devotion.

It was foolish to be jealous of a woman who wasn't even alive anymore. What on earth was wrong with her?

"Good night," she whispered. And before she could change her mind, she turned and climbed the stairs without looking back to see if he was still standing at the bottom, watching her.

Chapter Six

Lacey put her job search on the back burner for a few days and focused on Quinn and Amber. If it felt a little too personal, she ignored it. She was merely someone in a position to help a neighbor. While Quinn dealt with the insurance company and all the other details about the house repairs, Lacey cooked meals, did laundry, and one day after preschool she took Amber shopping for a new wardrobe. The first stop, though, was lunch at the diner. Shopping with a hungry and cranky kid was not part of the plan.

Every small town she could think of had a family restaurant where everyone knew everyone else and the daily specials were practically memorized according to the day of the week. In Gibson, the diner had the uninspired name of the Horseshoe Diner.

Amber was practically bouncing as they went inside. "I'm gonna have a hot dog and a chocolate milkshake!" she announced, her pigtails bobbing with each step. It was barely out of her mouth when she darted away. "Daddy!"

A jolt of something zipped through Lacey's body as her gaze followed Amber. Quinn was already at a booth, grinning at his daughter as if he hadn't seen her in days, rather than hours. Lacey was glad to see him, which made her a little uncomfortable. She'd thought today's lunch was just going to be her and Amber, not the three of them. She was trying to avoid the appearance of a family, which they definitely were not. But it was difficult when they lived under the same roof and as she started to care more and more for Amber. And for Quinn, a little voice in her head reminded her, but she pushed that thought away.

Pasting on a smile, she slid into the empty side of the booth. "I didn't realize you were going to be here," she said, putting her purse on the vinyl seat.

"I ended up having to come into town to sign some stuff," he replied. "I knew what time Amber was done, and I thought I'd meet you here."

"I want a hot dog, Daddy."

"Of course you do." He chuckled, the sound low and warm, sending ripples of pleasure over Lacey's nerve endings. Quinn really did have a great voice. Deep, quiet, but with a clarity and strength that…

Argh! She had to stop thinking this way. Instead she picked up the plastic menu and started scanning the offerings. She'd barely skimmed the first page when the waitress came over and asked to take their order.

"I'll have a hot dog and a chocolate milkshake, please," Amber ordered clearly, and Lacey hid a smile. For a girl her age, she had a lot of poise.

"What would you like on your hot dog, sweetheart?" The waitress was smiling too, at this point. Amber was hard to resist.

"Just ketchup. Please."

"You got it. How about you, Lacey?"

Lacey blinked, unsure how or why the woman knew her name. "Oh. Uh…"

The woman grinned. "You look a lot like your brother. You were in here a few days back, too, putting up your sign." She gestured with her pen towards the bulletin board. "Strangers don't stay strangers very long in this town."

"Oh. Right. I'll, uh…" She bit down on her lip. "I guess I'll have the chicken salad on whole grain with a side salad instead of fries."

"You didn't say please," Amber piped up.

Lacey swallowed. "Please."

Quinn was trying not to laugh as he ordered a cheeseburger platter with everything on it.

As they waited for their food, they were saved from much conversation as Amber chattered along, filling the silence with tales from preschool and how Taylor Johnson picked his nose and wiped it on his shirt and Madison Jeffries had picked up a baby snake on the playground. When the meals came, Lacey felt immediate buyer's remorse as she looked at her plate. Oh, there was nothing wrong with her sandwich or salad, but the sight of the rich milkshake and the savory scent of Quinn's burger had her mouth watering.

She looked up and saw Quinn watching her with a lopsided grin. Then he deliberately picked up a French fry, dipped it in the dish of ketchup on his plate, and bit into it with enthusiasm.

"Tease," she muttered, before she could think better of it.

His gaze held hers and there was that zing again. She hadn't meant it that way, but it seemed innuendoes happened without her even trying.

She picked up her fork and speared a piece of cucumber. This was better for her. She'd be glad of her choice in the long run. Right?

"So," she asked, "everything okay this morning?"

Quinn looked over at Amber and then back at Lacey. "Things have a tendency to move slowly, if you know what I mean."

She understood completely. Paperwork and bureaucracy moved on their own time, not anyone else's.

"How's your coverage?" She picked up half her sandwich and took a bite, then dotted her lips with her napkin. Amber, she noticed, already had an adorable smear of ketchup on the side of her mouth.

"Adequate...but it'll be tight for a while." He frowned. "A single income already makes it tight."

He looked over at Amber, and Lacey wondered how much of his paycheck was eaten up by preschool fees and after-school day care. He had a good job at Crooked Valley, but bringing up kids solo was an expensive venture. She didn't need her accounting degree to figure that one out.

"Anything I can do to help?" she asked.

"You're already doing it. I saw the pile of laundry this morning. You don't have to do that."

"I'm home. You're working. I might as well be doing something and if it helps you guys out, bonus." She smiled at him. "I'm not used to being idle, Quinn. I mean it. It's no bother."

Still, a load or two of laundry and running some errands with Amber didn't feel like much help. Lacey enjoyed being with the little girl, who said funny things through the innocence of a four-year-old filter.

They finished their meal and Quinn paid the bill, then

put on his hat. "Well, ladies, thank you for the lunch but I'd better get back to work."

"You can't go shopping with us, Daddy?"

Lacey grinned. She couldn't help it. Amber reminded her of a little Shirley Temple, hard to resist and twice as cute.

"Oh, I think that's best left to the women. You have fun and I'll see you at dinner."

"Lacey said she's making stuffy chops."

At Quinn's questioning glance, she elaborated. "Stuffed pork chops."

"Sounds good." They made their way outside into the sunshine and Lacey knelt down to help Amber get her thumbs into her mittens. When she stood up, Quinn was close. Too close.

"Thank you for this. I know you said it's no trouble, but I appreciate it just the same."

"You're welcome."

His hand was on the small of her back. She was sure it was just a polite gesture, mannerly. Gentlemanly. Still, the warmth of it seeped through her jacket to her skin.

Dry spell, she reminded herself. She only reacted to Quinn this way because she'd had such a big dry spell.

Even more disconcerting was the fact that he didn't seem to pick fights with her anymore. She sometimes missed the verbal sparring, but there had been bigger issues to deal with than the right way to load the dishwasher or whether or not to fold the towels in halves or thirds—the sort of thing they would have bickered about before.

His hand slid away.

"I'll see you at home?"

She nodded, but it suddenly became clear. She was

acting this way because she was pretending. She was playing house—with Quinn, with his daughter. But he was not her husband and Amber was not her child and it was certainly not her home…well, perhaps a third of it was, but that really didn't matter. She was playing house, pretending to have the life she had always wanted, but that had been taken away from her. She would have to watch that. Stay rational. Put things in perspective.

Crooked Valley was not growing on her. It certainly wasn't a permanent solution to her problems. After all, she couldn't live off her brother's goodwill forever, and she wasn't contributing to the ranch so she didn't expect any of the returns.

Quinn kissed Amber's head and jogged away to his truck. Lacey didn't want to get caught looking after him, so she took Amber's hand and put on her cheeriest voice. "Okay, sweetie. Let's hit the stores."

Much to Lacey's relief, Kailey Brandt phoned and said she'd like to meet to talk about some book work. The past few days had been busy, but Lacey knew she was getting too used to what were really housewife duties and she wanted something more. The last thing she needed to do was get in the habit of looking after Quinn and Amber as if they were her family. Once his house was fixed up, they'd be moving bac'k there and wouldn't need her anymore. Heck, they didn't need her now. They'd managed just fine, the two of them. It was her, needing to keep busy, longing to nurture, that kept her offering to do things for them. She was smart enough to know it. So the possibility of even part-time work was desperately exciting.

Quinn had driven Amber to school and was already

in the barn when Lacey tucked her hair into a messy topknot and put on her coat and boots. It was February, quite cold outside, and she had to take a few precious minutes to scrape the frost from her windshield. The roads were decent, though, and it only took a few minutes to drive from Crooked Valley to the Brandt place.

Brandt Bucking Stock was clearly a profitable operation. The fences and buildings were large and well-maintained, with fresh paint and a general neatness that spoke of consistent care. Lacey compared it to Crooked Valley and frowned a little. Perhaps Granddad had struggled to keep profits up towards the end. It wasn't that Crooked Valley was falling apart or anything, but it lacked the polish and prosperity of Brandt. The little details that perhaps Duke couldn't afford.

She parked in front of the house and grabbed her laptop bag. Before she could even get out of the car, Kailey appeared on the porch, zipping up a heavy jacket.

Lacey got out and slammed the door. "Good morning."

"Hey," Kailey replied. "The office is in the main barn, so come on down. I'll show you what's what."

They crossed the yard, heading towards the biggest building, white with dark green trim and massive sliding doors on one end. They entered through a smaller man door, and as they walked down the concrete corridor past long rows of stalls, Lacey was even more impressed. Kailey's boots made clicking sounds on the floor and Lacey noticed the woman's purposeful stride. She envied Kailey in that moment—sure of who she was and what she was doing. The woman was perhaps a few years younger than Lacey, but with far more confidence and purpose.

The barn office was nothing fancy; white walls with some framed pictures of different horses that Lacey assumed were Brandt stock, a shelf of trophies and cups, two large metal filing cabinets and a basic desk, chair and computer set up with a printer on a side table. In no time at all, Kailey had brought up the accounting and banking programs. It was all straightforward and simple, and a program that Lacey was familiar with. Everything was linked to make tax payments and payroll deductions as well as print checks.

"You've got a good setup here," Lacey said, clicking the mouse and checking out different parts of the programs. "Nothing jumps out at me as being strange or set up incorrectly, which is great. You say you've looked after it up until now?"

Kailey nodded. "I took an accounting course and learned the rest as I went along. I just don't like it." She grinned, the freckles on her nose bunching up as she scrunched it. "I'd rather focus on the business of running the breeding program. I've got my eye on a new stallion, but I haven't convinced the owner to sell him to me yet." Her eyes twinkled at Lacey.

"I can come in once a week if you like. Take care of your invoices and billing, run your payroll biweekly, pay the expenses. Shouldn't take me more than a few hours each time, more or less depending on what's going on and how busy you are."

"That'd be great!" Kailey looked so relieved Lacey laughed.

"Tell me about it. It's good to know I've finally got a little work lined up. I'm hoping I'll get a few more calls from the flyers I put around town."

"I figured Amber would have you dancing to her tune by now."

Lacey chuckled, leaning back in the chair. "Oh, she does. But she's gone all day, you know. As much as I grumbled about Quinn, he's not bad for a roommate. Keeps his stuff picked up. Worries about Amber getting in my way. Actually, it's kind of weird. It's like he goes out of his way to be nice to me."

Kailey's brows pulled together. "That's just Quinn, though. He's a really nice guy."

"Not to me." At Kailey's astonished expression, Lacey backpedaled. "That's not what I meant. I just mean… when we met he found fault with just about everything I did. Now he's so polite it sets my teeth on edge."

"Quinn never likes to inconvenience anyone. He has a hard time accepting help. The last thing he'd do is make things difficult. I'm actually surprised he agreed to stay at the house at all."

"I'm pretty sure he did it for Amber."

Kailey nodded. "So she'd have some consistency and familiarity. Quinn doesn't *not* like you, Lacey. He's not like that. He's just very protective of the life he's built. It's no secret that you're not really into the ranch, and for Quinn, Crooked Valley is the one thing that makes his life here possible, so nothing else has to change. You can't really blame the guy for being defensive."

And now she was throwing that into turmoil by being so stubborn. She still didn't want to be involved with the ranch, but maybe there was a way she could work something out for a while and then sell her third to Duke. It wasn't just Quinn who had something at stake with Crooked Valley. It was Duke and Carrie and their unborn child.

Lacey sighed. "You're not like that with me, though."

Kailey shrugged. "It's not my business at stake. Anyway," she continued, "there's going to be a benefit at the Silver Dollar on Valentine's Day. A local band is going to provide the music for free and all the cover charge money is going to give Quinn a hand. Not that we've told him, mind you. He'd say no to charity flat out. It's a surprise. At least until it's so far arranged that he can't say no."

A benefit? For Quinn? Lacey thought it was a lovely idea. Though the idea of it being on Valentine's Day struck her as a bit funny. Quinn wasn't the kind of guy who was looking for romance. Not when he was still stuck in his perfect past life...

And then she remembered the way their eyes had met at the bottom of the stairs and got that swirly, tingly feeling.

"Is there anything I can do to help?"

Kailey grinned and perched on the edge of the desk. "I thought you'd never ask. We'd like to hold a raffle on the night. Carrie agreed to look after getting some items, but we'd need someone to look after the cash. You, being the money person and all..."

"I should be able to do that."

"Great. I'll tell Carrie."

"What about Amber?" Lacey zipped up her bag and looked up at Kailey. "If it's at a bar, where will she go?"

Kailey smiled. "We have that all figured out. Amber's going to spend the night with her grandmother in Great Falls. Quinn takes her up there most Sundays anyway. They'll be able to manage for one night."

"You've got it all figured out."

"It's been in the works since the fire. That's what we do here. Look after our own."

Lacey wondered if she was considered "one of their own" or if she'd been gone too long. Joe Duggan had been a big part of this community, but that didn't necessarily extend to grandkids who hadn't given him the time of day.

"Well, just let me know what you need me to do and when."

"Of course."

"When would you like me to start with the books?" Lacey got up from the chair and put her bag on her shoulder.

"Day after tomorrow? Payroll is next week, so you can get the hang of the system before that. If that works for you."

Lacey smiled. "Lucky for you, my schedule is pretty wide-open."

Kailey walked Lacey back to her car, but before Lacey got in, the other woman put her hand on the window. "Lacey...don't say anything about this to Quinn, will you? He's so proud."

"I won't."

"He's been hurt a lot. Thanks for trying to help him out. I know it means a lot to him." She fidgeted for a second, shifting her weight on her feet before meeting Lacey's eyes. "Look, I don't want to pry into what's going on over at the ranch, but he's a good-looking guy and you're young and pretty and you're spending a crap ton of time together. I wouldn't want to see either of you hurt, and honestly I think Quinn has a ways to go before he's over Marie, you know?"

Lacey's face burned hot. "It's not like that..."

"I'm looking at you, Lacey, and I'm seeing that it could be. Just be careful. There's a little girl to think of, too."

Lacey's chin went up. "I know that. And it's really not like that, Kailey. I appreciate you wanting to protect him…"

"Not just him. Both of you."

"Well, that's kind of you. But there's nothing to worry about. I'm not going to be staying at Crooked Valley forever and before you know it, he'll be back in his house and it'll all go back to normal."

She smiled. Tightly. Felt like a complete liar even though she meant every word.

"I'm sure you're right." Kailey smiled back at her. A genuine smile. It hadn't been a warning or a threat. Kailey was simply looking out for someone she cared about, with concern and not jealousy or anger. She was a really nice woman, and Lacey wondered why Quinn hadn't snapped her up in a hurry. Clearly they were very close.

But perhaps Kailey was right. Quinn simply wasn't ready. Maybe he wouldn't be, not for a long time. Besides, a man like him deserved someone like Kailey, who was in the same business and liked the same things and could give Amber brothers and sisters. She wasn't capable of any of that.

"I'll see you later," she said quietly, and got into her car as Kailey stepped back.

As she drove away, she wished she could muster some resentment for their young, pretty neighbor. But it was hard to resent someone who was one hundred percent right.

THE MEETING WITH Kailey and trip to the Brandt operation got Lacey thinking. Who had been looking after the

Crooked Valley finances? Had Joe been doing it before he died? Was it Duke? Quinn? Was there a particular reason why the Duggan ranch didn't seem as prosperous as the Brandts'? She was home all day anyway. She could always take a look at the books.

She found Duke in the horse barn, in a stall with a big gelding who was currently standing patiently while Duke wielded a hoof pick. "Hey, brother."

He looked up briefly. "Hey, yourself. What brings you to the smelly part of the property?"

She laughed a little. Duke had never been one to mince words, mixing a bit of humor with the little barb of accusation. "Hey," she replied, "I don't actually mind horse smell. Much."

"Don't listen to her, Chief," he instructed the horse. "She doesn't mean to be insulting."

He let go of the foot and wiped the pick on his pant leg. "Seriously. What brings you to the barns? Is everything okay?"

She nodded, stepped back as he opened the stall door and came out into the corridor, latching the hasp behind him. "It's fine. I was over at Kailey's today. They're going to hire me to do some bookkeeping for them."

Duke's face lit up. "Hey, that's great!"

"Don't get too excited. I haven't had any other nibbles and it's only a few hours a week."

"Still. You have to start somewhere." He started walking down the corridor and she followed, all the way down to where the tack and feed were stored. There was a mini-office, nothing as big as at the Brandts', but with a bar fridge, coffeemaker, drop-leaf table and a few cast-off chairs, and behind that a half bath with a toilet and sink.

"You want a coffee?" he asked.

"Sure."

As Duke poured the black liquid from the pot—who knew how long the brew had been on the burner—Lacey grabbed a granola bar from a basket on the table. "Listen, Duke, I was wondering. Who does the books for the ranch?"

He turned around and put a mug in front of her, then took cream from the fridge and put it beside the cup. She added cream. A lot. It still barely changed the color of the coffee. She could hardly wait to see what it did to her stomach lining.

"Quinn, mostly. Apparently he was helping Joe with it for the last year or so, and took it on when Joe died. He's the manager. It made sense. Besides, I wouldn't know where to start."

He sat down across from her, took a sip of his coffee and winced. "Why? You offering?" His eyebrows went up hopefully.

"I thought I could take a quick look is all." She'd been hoping it had been Carrie or someone else paying the bills. Sure, she and Quinn had been getting along just fine. But if she started poking around in ranch business, she knew he'd have a few choice words for her.

It probably wasn't worth it.

"Never mind," she said, sitting back in the chair and eyeing the coffee with distrust. "I don't want to make waves. Quinn probably knows what he's doing."

"You worried about stepping on his toes?"

She raised an eyebrow. "Duh. We have this truce thing going on right now, considering we're living in the same house. It's for Amber's sake, really. I can just imagine he'd be really happy to hear me suggest improvements to the accounting system. Ten bucks says he'll say something like *we've always done it this way* and that'll be that. It's just…"

She halted, frowned.

"It's just what, Lace?"

She looked at her brother. He wasn't scowling. He was completely interested in whatever she was about to say.

"When I got to Kailey's, I could see the difference in the two places," she said honestly. "And it's not that Crooked Valley is run-down, by any stretch. But it doesn't look like the Brandts', either. It looks…tired. Is it because things fell behind as Joe got older? Finances? I just wondered if there was something there that could be adjusted so maybe…"

"I get what you're saying. It wouldn't hurt to have you take a look, anyway. Quinn's busy enough without having to do all the office work. If there's a way to make it easier…"

"No problem." She forgot her reservations about the coffee and took a long drink, shuddering at the bitter taste. "God, Duke. How long has that been on the burner?"

He shrugged. "I dunno. Since seven? Maybe eight?"

She pushed the cup aside. "Anyway, and it's not that I'm a big chicken or anything, but I think it would be better if you brought this up with Quinn. He's less likely to be defensive if it comes from you."

"I don't see why. If it were me, I'd be thrilled to have someone help out with the books."

"But it's not you. Look, Duke, this doesn't change anything. I'm still not interesting in owning a third of the ranch. Quinn knows it. It makes him defensive."

To her surprise, Duke stayed quiet. In fact, ever since she'd moved in, he hadn't pressed her about the ownership at all. Maybe he'd just been too preoccupied with work and his new bride and pending fatherhood that he'd let it go.

"Quinn loves this place. He's been here a long time."

Lacey huffed out a sigh. "He wasn't like that with you, though, was he? And you weren't going to stay here, either."

"I don't know what to say, Lacey. Besides, you guys seem to get along okay now."

"We came to a truce because of the current situation." Which was the truth, but not all of the truth. Not that she'd breathe a word to Duke. Wouldn't it be embarrassing for him to know that she actually *wanted* Quinn's approval?

Not that she'd admit it to anyone besides herself.

"If it makes you feel better, I'll talk to him about it later. Then the two of you can figure out a time to sit down and have a look at what's what."

"Okay. I'd better head back inside. Are you and Carrie coming for dinner tonight? I put pulled pork in the Crock-Pot. There's plenty."

"We'll see. I'll call up and let you know."

She was to the door before Duke's voice followed her. "Hey, sis?"

She turned around. "What?"

"Thank you. For looking after us, for looking after Quinn and Amber. For the record, Carter was a stupid ass to give you up. You care about people. You nurture them. He never appreciated that."

She swallowed tightly, touched by Duke's words, saddened, and on the verge of telling him the truth. But she couldn't somehow. Not that it was a big dirty secret or anything. It just made her feel like such a failure. Like such a…waste.

"Thanks, Duke. I really appreciate that."

"Anytime, shrimp." He winked at her, reverting to the nickname he'd given her when they were little kids. "I know I was gone for a long time, but I'm trying to make up for it now."

She'd forgotten what it was like to have a close family, to have a big brother to look out for her. It was a sweet, warm feeling. It stayed with her as she walked away and out of the barn. It was a feeling she dared not get used to, or else she might decide she didn't want to leave…

Chapter Seven

Quinn made his way from barn to house through a bitter wind that sent snow stinging against his cheeks. He'd taken Amber to school since the forecast was for random snow squalls throughout the day, but damn, it was only February and he was ready for spring. By spring—real spring—his house should be fixed and he and Amber could move back into their own home. He still hadn't told Amber the truth about their belongings. Most of them were gone. The smoke damage had been too intense. She'd been so upset about the fire in the first place that he hadn't wanted to add to her distress.

But it was hellish at times, staying here at Crooked Valley. It reminded him of things. Reminded him of how it used to be when he was married. For nearly two years he'd raised Amber on his own. He'd gotten used to having to cook meals, clean the house, do the laundry in addition to everything else. It wasn't that he didn't do those things before, either. He and Marie had shared the load. Always.

Sharing was different than being the only one left. Way different. And the truth was, it was really nice to come in after a long day and smell supper cooking and find a pile of fresh laundry on his bed. He didn't want to get too used to it. Lacey Duggan certainly wasn't here to take Marie's place. No one could do that.

The snow had drifted over the front steps again so he grabbed the shovel and cleared them off before stomping up the steps. He wasn't looking forward to the next hour. Lacey might be Martha Stewart around the house but she was still the woman who was not sticking around, who cared little about the ranch that was his livelihood. He was worried about Amber, too. He didn't want her to get too attached if Lacey was only going to leave again. Amber had been through more than enough.

The number one thing he'd tried to do since losing Marie was protect Amber from any more pain. Lacey was nice, and kind, and he owed her a lot for all her help. But what was best for Amber had to come first. The strange feelings that kept cropping up had to be tamped down. He didn't want to "move on" and even if he did it wouldn't be with someone who wasn't planning on sticking around.

Which made the task ahead even more unpalatable. Duke had asked him to show Lacey the books, to see if she could lend a hand. Duke had asked before if they should get a bookkeeper, but Quinn had refused. They didn't need to spend more money when he could do it himself.

Once she saw that they were just riding the line between red and black, she wouldn't want anything to do with the ranch for sure.

He walked in the door and was greeted by a smell that brought his mother's sour cream coffee cake to mind. It only made him more grouchy. Lacey was always baking something tasty, making herself indispensable. Hell, Amber thought the sun rose and set on her and talked about her more than her preschool teacher, whom she loved. It was just like when Lacey showed up here at Christmas. Perfect Lacey this, perfect Lacey that. The big difference was he'd been biting his tongue the past few weeks because she'd helped them so much since the fire. It would be damned rude to be anything but grateful. And polite.

In stocking feet, he stepped into the kitchen and saw the cake cooling on a rack. Clean dishes were stacked neatly in a drying rack in the sink, a damp tea towel forgotten on the countertop. He picked it up and folded it lengthwise before hanging it over the handle of the stove door. And then she stepped into the kitchen, carrying an empty laundry basket, and his heart did this weird dance in his chest.

Yeah, there was this, too. And it was damned inconvenient. Lacey Duggan was beautiful. It wasn't like he could help noticing. Especially since they were living in the same house.

She smiled when she saw him and it was like the room lit up. For God's sake, he was an idiot. They wanted entirely different things. She turned her nose up at what he valued and still, he saw her in a pair of fine-fitting jeans and a soft hoodie with her hair in a ponytail and his stupid body responded like a damned teenage boy. On the heels of those feelings came the heavy drag of guilt. Marie had been the love of his life and he was still mourning her. It wasn't fair that his body and mind kept betraying his heart by focusing on someone new.

"I'll be with you in a sec. Duke said you wanted to meet this morning so I could have a look at the books."

"I have some time."

"Let me just put this away." She headed for the laundry room at the end of the hall. "Did you know I'm going to be doing some accounting for Kailey?"

Her voice carried back and he let out a big breath. "No." Come to think of it, she might have mentioned it last night over dinner, but he'd been too preoccupied to pay much attention.

She came back, tightening her ponytail as she walked. "My first work since getting laid off. Hopefully it'll turn into a few more jobs as word gets around."

"And then what?" he asked.

She shrugged. "I don't know. I'll have to decide when the time comes."

"Are you still looking for full-time work?"

She frowned at him. "Of course I am."

"And so what if you move? What will you do with those clients you've set up?" She was looking at him funny, like he'd asked a ridiculous question. But it wasn't ridiculous at all. "Will you just leave them high and dry when you take off for your next job?" *Will you leave us high and dry too?* he thought. *Will my daughter cry at night again because someone else she cares about goes away?*

Lacey stepped back. "Quinn, would you like to do this another time?"

"No. Let's just do it and get it over with."

He knew he sounded short, but he was frustrated, dammit. Frustrated at not being in his own home, frustrated at all the work there was to do, frustrated that nothing ever seemed to be permanent. Why the hell did things have to change all the time?

And through all that frustration was Lacey, so young and pretty and more cheerful than he deserved, and he was starting to like her. Too much. And one day soon, she'd be gone, too. It was startling to realize that his days would go back to being somewhat gray and colorless when that happened.

Goddammit. He'd fallen under her spell as surely as Amber had. His daughter wouldn't be the only one to miss Lacey when she left, or when they moved back to their house. And that wasn't what he wanted at all. He wanted things back to normal!

"Do you want some cake?" she asked gently. "I could make you a cup of coffee, take it into the office."

"No, I damn well don't want any cake."

Her lips hardened and her eyes snapped at him. "Fine. Let's get this over with, then. Should be fun."

It was easier to deal with snippy, angry Lacey. Far easier than when she looked at him with soft eyes and full lips and that hint of pink in her cheeks.

Get a grip, he reminded himself. *Like she said. Get it over with.*

They went into the office and he went straight to the desk and hit the power button on the computer. While the old beast was booting up, he went to the first filing cabinet.

"This is where you'll find the paper files and records of invoices and receipts. The top drawer is this year's. Second drawer is last year's. Year before that was boxed up and put in the basement."

He shut the file cabinet door before she could really get a look inside. He'd forgotten how small the office was. And cold. While he logged on to the computer, Lacey went to the small space heater and flicked it on. "I see why you keep this in here," she said, rubbing her hands together. "It's chilly."

There was only one chair in the office, so she leaned

over his shoulder to look at the screen as he brought up files. The scent of her shampoo swam around him, all soft and floral, and he clenched his teeth.

He resented her. He appreciated her. And, as she rested a cool hand on his shoulder as she looked at the screen, he finally admitted to himself that he wanted her. He didn't want to. All of it fed into this big ball of confusion that was centered in the middle of his chest, like a weight pressing down on his collarbone, making it hard to breathe.

He cleared his throat and tried to ignore her hand. "So this is what we've brought in." He clicked another icon and brought up a second sheet. "Our expenditures are in this file."

She stood up straight and stared at the simplistic columns. "You mean to tell me you've been doing all this in a spreadsheet?"

"That's how Joe had it set up. He showed me. He'd run it that way for years."

"Clearly. That program's version is ancient. Why didn't you upgrade to accounting software?"

Of course, another criticism. That was just what he needed. "I'm a rancher, Lacey. Not an accountant."

"The new programs are easy to use, and you don't have to worry about copying and pasting stuff and making sure your formulas are correct. You enter it once, it posts it in the proper place and you can generate the right reports and everything. Heck, you can even direct file your taxes and stuff."

"And when would I have time to convert everything over and learn the program, huh? This is a working ranch. I've got my hands full just keeping things running around here and making sure we're in the black." He half turned in his chair and looked up at her. "At the end of the day everything balances. Isn't that what counts?"

"And that's great. It truly is. But…" She frowned at him. "I just thought…I'm staying here and not paying a bit of rent to Duke—"

"It's a third yours. Why would he charge you rent?"

"You take great pleasure in reminding me of that, don't you?" she answered, her words clipped. "I damn well know it's a third mine. You don't think I feel that pressure every day? That I don't feel some sort of obligation even though I want—" she broke off, shook her head. "Never mind. You wouldn't understand."

"Understand what?" He got up from the chair and faced her, his pulse quickening as the tension thickened in the small office.

"I need to stand on my own two feet! I need to stop feeling like life is happening to me and instead feel like I'm making it happen. I need to find my own job, pay my own bills, know that I'm not dependent on someone else for my happiness. For my…fulfillment."

They were incredibly different, so why did he feel like those words applied to him too? Particularly the part about relying on someone else for happiness.

"Is that what happened with your husband?" It was an intimate question but he asked it anyway. Just what sort of life had she had with him? He'd been putting snippets together here and there from what she said, from what Duke said.

"Yes. He checked out of our marriage and left me behind, picking up the pieces. And there were a lot of pieces. So I don't need reminding that I'm staying here on my brother's hopes that I won't leave, because once again it's not just my future at stake, it's his and yours and everyone else tied to Crooked Valley and if I can't figure out my own life, how the hell can I be responsible for someone else's?"

"Does it feel better to get that off your chest?" he asked, looking into her face. Her cheeks were flushed, her eyes sparked with anger and frustration. He shouldn't be finding her so attractive this way, but he couldn't deny his own body's response to her heightened state.

"Not really. You want to know why I asked Duke to approach you about the books rather than come to you myself? Because I knew this would happen. I know you don't think much of me, and you think I don't care. Whatever, Quinn. You've made up your mind, fine. But I was at Brandt yesterday and I couldn't help but compare this ranch to theirs and I wanted to know if the one thing I'm good at could help my brother. So sue me or yell at me or whatever. Just know that I'm not the one standing in the way here."

"Oh, that's rich." His blood heated again, annoyed by her accusation that any of this could be his fault. He'd been doing more than his share since Joe Duggan's health had started declining. He'd been thrilled when Duke had decided to stay on, because burning the candle at both ends and being a single parent was starting to take its toll. For her to accuse him of standing in the way of Crooked Valley's success was just ludicrous.

"I'll have you know I've been working this ranch for over ten years—"

"And that's great," she interrupted. "But heaven forbid you rely on anyone else, right? Or accept that someone might know more than you. Particularly someone you don't respect."

Her chest was rising and falling quickly, the sound of her breath audible in the silence that fell.

"You want to waltz in here and turn things upside down and then leave again. Excuse me if I don't get all excited about the possibility of having to clean up your messes."

"I don't want to turn things upside down at all! What are you talking about? I'm trying to help!"

Quinn stared at her and felt his frustration bubble up and over. There was just too much Lacey in his life all the time. In the morning when she made coffee and packed Amber's lunch for school. When she baked her stupid cakes and used her own stupid fabric softener on his clothes so he had her scent with him every damn day. Family dinners at night and the way she worked around the house while he took Amber through her bedtime routine. The little hesitation each evening when their eyes met and they said good-night before going to their separate rooms far too early, just to avoid time alone together...

"Maybe you could help a little less," he snapped. "I understand you're at loose ends and not working, but Amber and me? We're not your little project. We're not your surrogate family. So stop trying so goddamned hard to be indispensable to us. You're not Marie, so quit trying to be!"

She pulled back as if he'd struck her, her wide blue eyes filling with unexpected tears at the cruel words.

"Goddammit," he said as his control snapped. He stepped forward and cupped her head in his hands and kissed her, full-on, no holds barred, lips and tongues meshing in a furious, passionate dance.

Oh, God.

It had been so long since he'd held a woman in his arms, since he'd felt the softness of a female body pressed to his or heard a murmur of pleasure ripple through her mouth to his. She wasn't fighting him off, he realized, she was straining to reach him. Her fingers dug into his shoulder blades as she held him close and her teeth…oh God, her teeth bit into his lower lip, sending sparks of desire rocketing through him. He reached down, cupped one hand around a delicious buttock and pulled her against him, her gasp of surprise giving him a strange satisfaction as he ran his tongue over the seam of her lips.

He ground his pelvis against hers once, aching for her, but it was the one step that brought them both out of the passionate haze and into the present.

She pressed her hands to his chest—when had it started heaving like he'd been running? "Quinn," she whispered, her voice a mixture of wonder and apprehension. "What are we doing?"

He had to get a grip. "I'm sorry," he murmured, dropping his hands and backing up a step, needing to put some distance between their bodies in an attempt to clear his head.

"I…" She looked at him, her eyes wide and wary. "I never tried to replace your wife." Her lower lip quivered. "I know how much you loved her. Everyone says so. I swear I just wanted to help."

"I'm sorry I said that," he replied roughly, meaning it. "That's my own frustration and I shouldn't take it out on you." His own frustration indeed. It had been a year and a half. Why did he feel disloyal? It wasn't reasonable to think he'd go through the rest of his life alone.

To think that he wouldn't care for someone again. That wasn't logical.

But once more, his heart got in the way. And once more, he realized that there was more than his heart at risk here. It was Amber's, too. Amber, who clearly needed her mother so much. If this went anywhere, and ended badly, she'd be so hurt.

"Then the kiss was…" Lacey's voice whispered through the room, soft and uncertain.

He swallowed. Admitting he was sexually drawn to her would be like dropping a match on gasoline. He was in no position to leave Crooked Valley and neither was she. There was really only one thing to do, and that was lie. Something he was never comfortable with, but which he knew was necessary for all their sakes.

"Frustration. Again, I'm sorry. It was unfair of me."

He would swear she looked relieved and disappointed all at the same time. Had she been feeling the same pull as he had? It seemed impossible, but she'd definitely participated equally in the kiss, practically wrapping herself around him…

Down, boy.

Accounting. He had to get back to thinking about numbers and columns.

"About the books," he said, turning around and looking at the computer screen which was now a floating mass of bubbles as the screensaver took over. "Have a look. Convert them if you want. When the time comes for you to go, I'll hire some part-time help to keep them up to date. Or maybe you can teach Carrie. As her pregnancy progresses and then after the baby's born, she'll be spending less time as foreman."

He didn't look at her again. Couldn't. He just spun

on his heel and left the room, grabbed his jacket and boots and headed out to the barns. Anything to get some breathing room and get his head on straight again.

He wanted to say that the kiss had affected him the most. It would be easier, because it was purely physical.

But that wasn't what stuck in his mind right now. It was how hurt she'd looked when he'd accused her of insinuating herself into his life. And that told him one disturbing fact: more than his libido was involved where Lacey Duggan was concerned.

And that was troubling indeed.

Chapter Eight

Lacey examined the expenditures column once more, matching them to invoices and looking at ways to streamline some of the administrative costs of the ranch. As far as operational costs, she'd made a list of potential items to ask Duke about, since she knew very little about the actual ranching aspect. Clearly Quinn wasn't interested in being involved, and she wasn't going to force it. Especially after that kiss.

She sighed, slid her hand off the mouse and stared blindly at the monitor. The kiss. It had been surprising, passionate, glorious, magnificent. She hadn't imagined Quinn had that kind of raw intensity, but there had been nothing soft or tentative about how he kissed her. It had thrilled her right to her toes, leaving her breathless and off balance.

Just thinking about it sent a spiral of desire whipping through her.

But Quinn wasn't interested. He was frustrated, he'd said. And unhappy with himself for doing it.

Way to make a girl feel great.

She inhaled deeply and put her hand on the mouse again, determined to get through this section of the accounting today. Quinn didn't want her here. He accepted her help because he needed it, not because he wanted it—or her. Fine. She'd clean up the books for Crooked Valley, and throw herself into her employment efforts again. Something that took her away from the house. If she were lucky, she'd find something in Great Falls and she'd be able to move out and really start over rather than feeling like a mooch.

Quinn picked Amber up from day care and for once the bubbly chatter of the little girl didn't lift Lacey's spirits. Supper was an unusually quick fix of what Lacey's mom had inaccurately called goulash—ground beef, macaroni and tomato soup. If Quinn noticed the change in effort, he said nothing, and Amber ate it up without a complaint, as long as there was lots of grated cheese to go on the top.

Quinn wouldn't meet her eyes.

After the dinner mess was cleaned up, Lacey disappeared back into the office. Once more, Quinn didn't interfere. If he assumed she was working on Crooked Valley stuff, all the better. Tonight she was sending emails and making phone calls about the benefit dance for Quinn. Before, she'd thought it was a nice thing to do, but after today, it meant that the sooner the money was raised, perhaps the faster they'd get back in their house and not be in each other's hair all the time. Right now Lacey was thinking if she had anywhere else to go…

But she didn't. So the easiest solution was getting Quinn back in his old place.

Amber popped in to say good-night, and Lacey's heart gave a bittersweet pang as she realized how much she'd come to love the little girl. She kissed her clean hair and said "Good night, honey."

Amber was nearly to the door when she spun back.

"Lacey? Will you help me with my Valentines tomorrow? My teacher gave me a list with the names in my class but I's still learning my letters."

If things had gone according to plan with Carter, they might have had a daughter like this. It seemed like the muscles in her abdomen tightened, a reminder of what could never be. She could never carry a child of her own. God knows she'd tried. The hysterectomy had pretty much taken care of any of those hopes.

"Of course I'll help you," she answered softly, knowing she couldn't take her dissatisfaction with Quinn out on Amber.

"Our party is Friday," Amber added with a quicksilver grin. "I told my teacher I would bring cookies."

Of course she did. And she knew just how to wrap Lacey around her little finger, too. Not that Lacey minded. Not this once.

"We'll talk tomorrow. Your daddy is waiting to take you to bed."

"Okay. Night, Lacey."

When she was gone, Lacey put her head in her hands, bracing her elbows on the desk. What a mess. Why had she allowed her emotions to get involved? She was supposed to be here to start over. Not get attached to a family that was not her own. She'd worried about not getting along with Quinn at the beginning. Now it was…it was just too much.

She could do this. All she had to do was stay rational, logical. There was nothing wrong with liking Quinn's daughter. She was Duke's sister, after all. Even if she didn't take on her part of the ranch, she could be a part of the circle that made up Crooked Valley.

Except the circle as they all knew it might not even exist if she went her own way.

"If?" she murmured in the quiet office. Where had that word come from? Up until now it had been *when*.

Darn. She sat back in the chair and blew out a breath. Duke had been smart after all. He'd known, hadn't he? That once he got her here, in the house, it'd be hard for her to leave. Once she saw the people, the life…

He was sneaky, her brother.

She'd driven into the Brandt spread and found herself making comparisons. Gone headfirst into the books and gotten a fair picture of all that went into the running of a cattle operation. She cared. She cared whether it succeeded or failed.

And she didn't want to be responsible for it being sold out from under her brother, not when he'd made a whole new life here for himself. He had a wife. A baby on the way. And he was happy. Could she really ruin that just so she could be right?

After hitting save, she shut down the computer and went out into the hall, found her boots and jacket and started pulling them on. Upstairs a door closed and then Quinn appeared, coming quietly down the steps. Her heart jumped simply at the sight of him. He might be able to ignore what happened between them, but she could not.

"It's late to be going out," he said softly, looking back upstairs and then at Lacey again. She avoided meeting his gaze directly, not wanting to get sucked into the depths of his eyes. That happened all too easily.

"I'm just running down to Duke's for a minute. Leave the door unlocked. I'll lock up when I come back."

"Okay."

She zipped up her coat and pulled on a pair of thick mitts.

"About today…" he began, but she held up a hand.

"It's okay. You said what you needed to. I'm fine, Quinn." She couldn't help it, she met his gaze. "If anything, it woke me up to reality. So don't worry about it."

"Reality? What does that mean?"

She swallowed tightly, wondering what to say, how much to reveal. "I think we've both been wondering, don't you? Now we've got it out of our system. We can forget about it and move on. Focus on what's really important."

He frowned. "Like what?"

"Like Crooked Valley. Like me finding a full-time job. And you need to worry about getting your life back to normal. For Amber."

His cheeks flushed a little. "Yes, for Amber," he agreed. "I have to think of her first. I don't want her getting too attached to you if you're just going to leave again. She doesn't need disappointments."

It was honest but damn, it smarted. "Right. Well, anyway, I'm going to pop in and see Carrie and Duke for a bit. Don't wait up. Just leave the porch light on when you go to bed."

She sent him the most platonic, impersonal smile she could before turning the knob and pulling the door open. She closed it behind her with a soft click, inhaled the cold air deeply into her lungs.

The ground was hard under her feet as she made her way to the bunkhouse, which now served as Duke and Carrie's home. It was a small two-bedroom bungalow, big enough for the two of them, or even the three of them once the baby came. She knew Duke had plans to build a piece on as their family grew. She'd asked him once about moving into the big house since he and Carrie were planning kids, but they'd both agreed they liked where they were. Or so they said.

Carrie answered the door, a smile blossoming on her face when she saw Lacey standing there. "We were just talking about you!" she exclaimed, standing aside so Lacey could enter. "Duke was saying you were going to take a look at the books."

Lacey almost wished she hadn't said yes to Kailey's job offer, because then she wouldn't have asked about Crooked Valley and she could have gone on with her original plans. Funny how one thing could change everything…

Kind of like Quinn's kiss.

She put that to the back of her mind and smiled at her sister-in-law. Carrie wasn't really showing yet, though Lacey noticed she was wearing leggings and a baggy sweatshirt. Her waistbands were probably getting a little tight now that she was at the end of her first trimester.

Lacey would not be jealous. She would not be bitter. She would not.

"Is Duke around? I wanted to talk to you guys about something."

"Sure. We were just watching some TV, but it's nothing we're too interested in. Do you want some tea or anything?"

"I'm okay."

"Hey, is that Lace?" Duke's voice echoed from the living room.

"Yeah, it's me," she called back. Grinning, she toed off her boots and hung her jacket on a hook behind the door. "On second thought, Carrie, do you have anything stronger than tea?"

Carrie chuckled. "Not much. There might be a beer in the fridge."

"That works for me. I could stand to kick back for a bit."

The house was warm and cozy, Carrie's feminine touches evident in the decor. Duke was sitting on the sofa, the cushion next to him vacant except for a light blanket. They'd been cuddling in front of the television, and Lacey thought that was lovely.

"You," she accused, right off the bat, "are a sneaky devil."

He feigned an innocent look. "What did I do?"

She plopped down on a side chair. "You knew, didn't you? You knew that once I got here, I'd get roped into this place."

"Really?" He looked so hopeful she nearly laughed. Instead she let out a grudging sigh.

"Yes, really." Carrie came back with her drink. "Thanks, Carrie," she said, taking the bottle into her hands. "Anyway, I want to run some hypotheticals past you. Maybe there's a way we can find some middle ground so we both get what we want."

Duke sat up a bit. "I'm intrigued."

"Me, too," Carrie said, resuming her seat beside Duke.

Lacey wasn't entirely sure where to begin. "I'm just figuring this out, so don't assume too much, okay? What I need tonight is a sounding board."

"Okay," they both agreed, then looked at each other and smiled.

It made Lacey lonely, seeing that level of togetherness. She took a sip of her drink and licked her lips, searching for the right words to start. In the end, it came down to a simple truth.

"I don't want you to lose Crooked Valley."

"That's good to know," Duke responded, and Lacey blew out a breath.

"I think it's stupid, the way Granddad split this up, but there's nothing we can do about it. I don't want to be the cause of you losing it, Duke. You and Carrie love it here, and you're making your life here. I'm thinking there has to be a way for me to work the conditions in my favor, so the ranch doesn't get put up for sale and I don't have to wade my way through this place with mud on my boots." She looked over at Carrie and smiled. "Not that there's anything wrong with that, if it's your thing."

Carrie smiled back.

"Do you have any ideas?"

She nodded. "I think we need to have a lawyer take a good look at the will, for one thing. It will tell us how involved I have to be to meet conditions. I can't believe Granddad would expect me to be a rancher. I'm not even that comfortable around horses. But I'm good with numbers and computers. If being the ranch bookkeeper satisfies the terms, I'd be willing to stay on in that capacity. I think I could help Crooked Valley streamline some of the costs, and take advantage of a few tax breaks that I'm not sure Joe even knew about. It might give you some financial breathing room, especially as things need to be repaired and you're expanding your family."

Duke's brows lifted. "Lacey, that's great! I'd love that, I really would."

"I'm already doing some of the bookkeeping for Kailey's family, and I could do ours even if I got a full-time job somewhere close. Which brings me to the next bit."

"There's more?"

This was actually harder, she realized. She'd come to love the big house, the spacious kitchen, cozy fireplace, big bedrooms. "There's the question of where I'll live."

Duke's gaze held hers. "We're happy here. You should stay in the house."

But Lacey shook her head. "Duke, it's too big for just me. I mean, Quinn and Amber are there now, but that's not exactly a comfortable situation and they'll be going back to their own place when their house is ready. Besides, what if I find a job in the city or something? It's a long commute from here. Even finding a place on the other side of Gibson would cut fifteen or twenty minutes off my commute each way. You and Carrie should have the house. It's meant to be filled with kids and laughter and toys and family."

It hurt to say that last bit, even though it was true.

Duke's face softened, his eyes filled with understanding. "Lacey, I know it doesn't seem like it now, but you'll have that someday. Just because things didn't work out with Carter…"

"No, I won't," she answered firmly. Perhaps it was time to stop dancing around the subject. "Duke, you had to adjust to losing your hearing in one ear. It wasn't just the hearing, it was how it affected your life in the military. Your decisions that came afterwards. That was tough, right?"

"You know it was," he agreed. "I have to make adjustments all the time."

"And it won't ever be better, not even someday."

Carrie leaned forward. "What are you trying to say, Lacey?"

"The real reason Carter left…why things fell apart is because I can't have children. When I couldn't get pregnant, the doctors discovered endometriosis. We tried a few different things, but in the end I had a hysterectomy. I'll never fill the big house with kids, you see. It should be you."

Duke's mouth had fallen open while Carrie's face drooped with dismay. "Oh, Lacey, I'm so sorry." Her cheeks pinkened. "It must be so hard for you when I…" Awkward silence filled the room.

"I don't begrudge you one ounce of your happiness," Lacey whispered, her voice hoarse. "It's hard sometimes, but I'm really trying to move on. I don't want you guys to lose this place, and I'll help you keep it, but I have to take charge of my own life. Make my own decisions. So if I take on some of the office and administrative duties works, and if I can live off-site, we might be able to give this a go."

There were a few beats of silence before Duke asked, "What does Quinn think about this?"

Just the mention of his name made her muscles tense, in good ways and bad. "It's not up to Quinn. I know he's your manager, but the terms of the will and the ownership of the ranch is really about us."

"I value his opinion, Lacey. He's been doing this a lot longer than me."

She was rather tired of Quinn being held up as this paragon of perfection. It seemed like he could do no wrong. Perfect at his job, perfect dad, perfect husband. It was an impossible standard to live up to.

"Quinn is more than happy to pass on the accounting, that I can tell you for sure. As far as the rest goes, I know for a fact that what he really cares about is Crooked Valley and making sure he still has a job. This will take care of that. Or at least I hope it will." Quinn would be able to move back to his house, keep his job, support himself and Amber. Have the life he wanted to have.

Except he'd rather have it with Marie. His wife. Despite the kiss today, Lacey knew one thing for sure. Quinn was a long way from being over the woman he'd loved. After feeling like such a failure with Carter, Lacey wasn't interested in trying to compete. Quinn wasn't the only perfect one in that relationship and there was no way Lacey wanted to try to live up to Marie's memory.

She needed to find a job and a new place to live. Like, yesterday.

"I'll call the lawyer first thing in the morning, so we can iron out particulars. Then it's just a matter of getting Rylan onboard."

Lacey gave a wry chuckle. "Rylan, with his wandering feet? Good luck. He's not the settling down type."

"I never thought I was, either. Until I landed here. I think Granddad knew what he was doing more than we gave him credit for."

Lacey pondered that for a moment. "Do you think we would have stayed here if Dad hadn't died?" Those days were a hazy memory for her; she'd been very young when their father had been killed in action. The ranch life hadn't been for their mom, Helen, and she'd moved into the city where she could work and provide for them all.

Duke shrugged. "Who knows? Does it matter? We're here now. And I, for one, am glad to be connecting with my family again."

"Even Mom and David?" It was no secret that Duke hadn't been a big fan of their mother remarrying.

"Even David. He ended up being a decent guy at Christmas. He makes her happy."

Lacey's eyes misted over. "Wow. Kudos to you, Carrie. Love has made this big lump into a bit of a marshmallow."

"What can I say?" Carrie replied, taking Duke's hand in hers. "He did the same for me. And someone is out there for you, too. I really believe that. The kids thing doesn't have to be a deal breaker."

"I'm afraid it does," Lacey answered, her voice suddenly brittle. "At least to some people."

"Then he didn't deserve you," Duke decreed. "You need a better man. Someone like…"

"Don't even think about saying it." She was terrified he would try to set her up or even worse, that *Quinn* was the name sitting on his tongue.

Duke just laughed. "Okay. Fair enough. Lacey, I'm really glad you came over. Glad you're willing to give this a shot. Thank you. I mean it."

She took another long drink of her beer and relaxed back into the cushions. "Honestly? Gibson isn't such a bad town. The people are nice. And now I have family here. Despite the employment situation, I could have landed in worse places."

Carrie laughed. "I had to convince Duke of that, too."

Lacey turned the bottle around in her hands. "Just one thing, though. Don't mention any of this to Quinn, okay?"

"Why?" Duke frowned, his brows pulling together. "I thought you said he was onboard with you doing the accounting?"

"He is. It's just…complicated. We don't see eye to eye on a lot of stuff. I'd rather just not get into it until I know for sure what I'm doing, you know?"

Carrie and Duke shared a look that Lacey couldn't quite interpret, but she could tell they were hesitating. "Look, it's been challenging being roomies, okay? I came to you because you're my brother. I need to figure this all out without Quinn putting in his two cents."

"And you think he would?"

She nodded quickly. "Oh, I know he would. He has opinions about everything I do."

She saw Carrie give Duke's hand a squeeze, and the topic was miraculously dropped. Instead, Carrie changed the subject to the benefit. "Speaking of, how are things coming along for the dance at the Silver Dollar? Kailey said you'd taken on getting some items for a raffle."

The conversation turned to planning the event and the three of them stayed up far later than was wise, but Lacey left with a full heart. Somehow, in the space of a few weeks, Crooked Valley had started to feel like a home. And she knew it had little to do with location and a lot more to do with family and acceptance. Maybe Granddad had known that all along, too.

Maybe Joe Duggan had been smarter than any of them had given him credit for.

Chapter Nine

As resolved as Lacey was to keep her distance and perspective where Quinn was concerned, she wasn't so good at it when it came to Amber. The girl was just too cute, even when she got frustrated with writing the names on her Valentines and put down her pencil in disgust. They took a break and chatted about what kind of cookies Amber wanted for her class party. Quinn might puff and bluster about Lacey usurping Marie's place, but Lacey wasn't about to deny Amber a few cookies for her first Valentine's Day party. Quinn certainly didn't have time for it and grabbing ones from the grocery store just wasn't the same.

During the day, though, she worked in Quinn's office when he was in the barns, converting the accounts over to the new program. She spent one morning at the Brandt ranch, and met with two other prospective clients in town. Her full-time inquiries garnered two new interview appointments. Maybe the argument with Quinn was exactly the kick in the pants she'd needed to really find her gumption. Up until then she'd just been going through the motions.

Signs had gone up around town, advertising the Valentine's Day event, with no mention of the proceeds

going to the Solomons. It amazed Lacey that the secret hadn't got out and back to Quinn, but he seemed to
know nothing about it. The biggest challenge, it seemed,
was going to be actually getting him to go. That bit was
Kailey's job, a detail for which Lacey was grateful to
have been spared.

February 13th rolled around and Amber and Lacey
spent the afternoon making tiny heart-shaped chocolate
shortbreads. As the cookies cooled, they decorated them
with pink icing and left them to set a bit before packing
them in cookie tins for the next day's event.

Lacey looked around the messy kitchen and realized
it was going to be harder than she expected, leaving this
house. It felt like a house should feel—warm and welcoming. Of course that could all change when Quinn and
Amber left again. It wasn't really made for one person.
If she moved out, and Quinn went back home, the big
house would be empty again.

"There," she said, dusting her hands off on her apron.
"That's the last pan in the oven. And there are extra.
What do you say, should we taste test?"

"Yes!" Amber bounced up and down on her toes,
then looked at Lacey speculatively. "How many extra?"

Lacey burst out laughing. "Enough for you to have
two and no more or you'll ruin your supper."

"Okay." Amber made a close examination of the cookies and plucked two off the rack. Lacey expected her to
pop the cookies in her mouth but instead she hopped off
the stool, came around the counter and handed them to
Lacey. "These ones are yours," she stated, then popped
back around to choose her own.

"Thanks," Lacey said, and waited until Amber was
ready, then they took their first bites together.

Crumbs flaked away from the buttery cookie onto the floor. "Yummy," Amber said, breaking into a crumb-and-frosting smile. She licked her lips and looked at Lacey with pure adoration. "Lacey, I wish you were my mama."

The innocent words were a shock to Lacey's heart. A yearning so powerful, so pure, enveloped her and for a fleeting moment, she wished it, too. But being Amber's mom would mean being Quinn's wife and that simply wasn't going to happen. "Oh, honey," she murmured, and went over and put her arm around the little girl. "That is such a sweet thing to say. I can't be your mama, but I'll always be your friend, okay?"

"But why can't you be my mama?" Amber peered up at her with curious eyes. "You already do what mamas do. You wash my clothes and do all the cooking and tidy the house and make Valentimes cookies and you love me, too, right?"

Lacey sighed, so torn and yet happy, too. "I do love you. And don't you forget it. But to be your mommy, I'd have to be married to your daddy, see?"

Amber shrugged. "So marry my daddy." Unconcerned, she started putting decorated cookies on the bottom of the big tin.

How on earth could Lacey answer that? She was just trying to figure it out when the front door opened. Great. Just what she needed. Quinn. Instead of answering Amber, Lacey went to the sink and started piling up dishes to be washed.

Quinn entered the kitchen, the top of his hair flattened from his hat, his shoulders looking impossibly broad in a soft denim shirt. "Cookies?" he asked, looking at Amber, sparing Lacey a brief glance before smiling at his daughter.

"Lacey helped me for my party tomorrow," Amber explained.

"I see."

Lacey heard the strain in his voice. Remembered how he'd told her to back off trying to replace Marie. She knew she should let it go but somehow couldn't. "Amber asked if I'd help her make cookies. It's her first Valentine's Day party."

The warning was issued: *don't make a big deal out of this, I did it for your kid.*

But Amber, being four, didn't sense the undertones and picked up a cookie. "Lacey said there's extras. Here." She pressed it against his lips, and with a laugh he opened his mouth so she could pop it inside.

He was still chewing when Amber went back to her cookie-packing and said, matter-of-factly, "I asked Lacey if she'd marry you and be my mama. Is that okay, Daddy?"

Lacey knew she should not feel quite so gratified when crumbs caught in Quinn's throat and he started coughing.

He looked over at her, eyes watering, crumbs on his lips and she struggled not to laugh. He would not find this funny. But he looked so comical, all red-faced and watery-eyed with the odd crumb flying out of his mouth when he coughed.

Amber, God love her, was waiting patiently for him to finish.

Lacey quietly handed him a glass of water which he took, drank, and finally breathed normally.

"So?" Amber persisted. "Can Lacey be my mama?"

Quinn's face flattened as his expression turned serious. "Honey, it's not that simple."

Amber's little eyebrows puckered in the middle. "It's easy. You ask her to marry you and she says yes and then she's my mama. Lacey said she would marry you."

Lacey's stomach clenched but she kept her voice soft and soothing. "Sweetie, that's not what I said. I said that while I love you, I can't be your mama because I'm not married to your daddy. We'd have to love each other for that to happen."

Amber's eyes filled with tears. "You don't love my daddy?"

Oh, God. She went to the child and knelt down in front of her. "You have the best dad ever, Amber. But we are just friends. We're not...like the princess and that ice guy in the movie you like so much, know what I mean?"

"But I want you to!" The tears in Amber's eyes spilled over and Lacey's heart broke. It was hard to be mad at Quinn for his stance the other day. This sort of thing was exactly what he was trying to avoid. She only wished he'd believe her when she said she wouldn't hurt Amber for the world.

"I know," Lacey answered softly. "And you can't know how happy it makes me to know you would like for me to be your mom. It's the biggest compliment ever. But like I said, I don't have to be your mama to be here for you. Right?"

Amber nodded halfheartedly.

Quinn came over and said quietly, "Come here, chicken." When Amber turned, he hefted her up into his arms and folded her into a quick hug. "So, are you okay now? Do you understand what Lacey said?"

She nodded, tucking her head into the curve of his

neck. Quinn looked at Lacey over top of Amber's head. Lacey was sure she'd never seen him look so bleak.

He reached into his jacket pocket. "Look what I picked up today. Do you want to watch it?"

Lacey saw the red cover of a DVD case and recognized it as the Charlie Brown Valentine special. "Oooh, a Valentine's Day DVD!" she exclaimed, perhaps a bit too brightly but desperate to change the subject and mood. "Go put it in, sweetie. You can watch it before dinner."

"Okay." Amber took the case from her dad and made her way to the living room, where, like most kids her age, she was completely proficient in running the DVD player.

"What the hell was that?" he whispered, low enough for Amber not to hear but enough for Lacey to detect the ire in his voice.

"I had no idea, I swear. One moment we were baking cookies and the next she sprung it on me. I was trying to explain when you came in."

"Where on earth would she get such an idea?"

It burned that he considered the idea so utterly implausible. Was she really that terrible? That unattractive and unappealing?

"I certainly didn't put it there," she responded, with a fair bit of acid in her voice. She turned away and went to the sink, flicking on the taps to run water for the dishes, hoping he couldn't tell how much his words stung.

But the running water only served to camouflage their voices as Quinn followed her. "This was what I was afraid of. She's too attached to you. And now she's going to get hurt."

"I would never hurt her! Wow, you must really think a lot of me."

"Hey, I know you're not staying around. You're only here temporarily, and then you'll be gone and where will Amber be? Hurt. She needs stability, not someone who is in her life and out of it again."

Words sat on her lips, begging to be spoken. It was entirely possible she would be staying in Gibson or at least close by for the foreseeable future.

And then she looked at Quinn and the defensive expression tightening his face and she understood. He wasn't just talking about Amber. It wasn't Lacey who was in and out of their lives, it was Marie. And because Marie had left them both, he didn't trust anyone to stay.

He didn't want any disappointments, either. Which meant that maybe, just maybe, he cared for her more than he was letting on.

Her anger towards him dissipated.

"Yes, she needs stability," she agreed softly. "Which is why she has you, and Duke, and Carrie and Kailey and everyone who has always been a support to you."

"But none that she's latched on to like you," he answered, turning a bit so that his back blocked them from Amber's view.

"Quinn, I don't know what to say. Except even if we don't live in the same house much longer, I'll still care about her and want to see her and be there for her."

"Until you leave."

"What if I didn't leave?"

His eyes widened. "What do you mean?"

She peered around his shoulder and saw Amber engrossed in the show. "I mean, even if I'm not right here, at Crooked Valley, I've decided to stay in the area."

"When were you going to tell me?"

She met his gaze. "When I had figured out all the

logistics." In other words, without his input and opinions, which always seemed to cloud any sort of clarity she managed to achieve. There was something between them. The kiss had proved that. Whether or not it ever went any farther was up in the air. This was one decision she had to make on her own, for the right reasons.

She could see the wheels turning in his head. The two of them, in the same town, either snapping at each other or gazing into each other's eyes like idiots, just like they were doing now. She'd thought of it, too, and didn't have the answers.

"I care about your daughter, Quinn. I know what you said about getting too close, but I couldn't say no when she asked for help with the cookies. Please don't be angry at me for that."

"I'm not, and I'm sorry I snapped at you. The truth is, I'm angry at myself for not being able to spare her disappointments. As a parent, the worst thing ever is seeing your child in pain." He sighed. "You'll understand that someday when you have your own."

But she wouldn't. And there was one little girl who'd like to have her for a mom and she couldn't do that, either. What little composure she'd been hanging onto, crumbled.

"Lacey? Did I say something wrong?"

She shook her head quickly and turned back to the dishes so he wouldn't see the distress on her face.

But he wouldn't let it alone. Leave her alone. "Now you know why I said what I did the other day…"

"No," she replied, starting to lose her cool. "No, I don't. I'm not trying to be your sainted wife, Quinn. I wasn't then, I'm not now. And the last thing I want is to be compared to her, okay?"

And then her heart stuttered a bit, because she was afraid if he did compare her to Marie, she'd come up sorely lacking. Her ego had taken a big enough beating when she wasn't "woman enough" for Carter. If Quinn actually verbalized her inadequacies to her face, she'd fall apart a little. Or a lot.

She bit down on her lip and scrubbed at a mixing bowl, hating that after everything, his opinion still seemed to matter. It wasn't fair.

"I'm just trying to protect my daughter," he murmured, "from getting hurt more than she already has."

She turned glistening eyes to him. "And I resent that you think she needs protecting from me. That either of you do. Just go, please. Let me clean up this mess before her show finishes and she sees me upset."

He left her alone and she nearly wiped the finish off the dishes, she scrubbed so hard with the dishcloth. By the time Amber's show was finished, the kitchen was spick-and-span and Lacey had to get out. If Amber said anything more about motherhood, Lacey was pretty sure she'd lose it. And she definitely wasn't up for another emotionally-charged conversation with Quinn.

She found him in his office and stuck her head in the door. "I have plans in town for supper. You and Amber can take something out of the freezer."

"We'll be fine," he answered briefly. "We managed before. You don't have to worry about us."

She wasn't sure if it was meant to be a reassurance or a brush-off, but she knew how it felt. *We don't need you. We're fine without you.*

You don't matter.

"Bye," she replied, and stepped away.

One of the hardest things she'd ever done was walk

away from the house that evening, but she knew it was necessary. It was time to put some real distance between them all. One thing was for sure. As much as it hurt Lacey, she'd rather that than cause any more pain to the precious girl inside who'd lost enough already.

THE LAST THING Quinn wanted to do was go out for Valentine's Day. How he'd been roped into attending some cockamamy dance at the Silver Dollar, he wasn't sure, but it definitely seemed like the universe was conspiring against him. His mom had called and asked if Amber could come visit and sleep over today, because she had plans on the weekend and wanted to do something special for Valentine's Day with her granddaughter. He couldn't say no—Amber loved visiting her grandma. But that left him alone on the most romantic night of the year. Torture for singles. He'd planned on grabbing a frozen pizza for his supper and hiding out at the house. Hopefully without Lacey in his way.

Now he was patting on some aftershave and tucking his favorite blue-and-white-striped shirt into clean jeans, making sure the cuffs were buttoned over his forearms. The bandages were gone, but he was still a little self-conscious about the pink scars on his skin, which would fade more but never really go away completely.

He wished he was better at saying no. Kailey had called. She'd had plans to go to the dance at the saloon and her date had cancelled at the last minute. Her argument had been that it was less pathetic to go as friends, as they'd done before, than sit home alone. When she learned that Amber was already cared for, any argument he might have put up didn't have a leg to stand on.

Even Lacey had plans. She'd gone straight from a

job interview to dinner with friends. At least that was what her note said.

He turned off the bathroom light and sighed. Maybe it was better to get out tonight. He had to start doing that more, and at least with Kailey there were no expectations. What else was he going to do, sit home and wallow? That would only lead to thinking about a certain stubborn woman with coppery curls and snapping blue eyes. Why couldn't he get her out of his mind?

Kailey wasn't quite ready when he arrived at the Brandt spread, so he waited in the kitchen, talking to her mom and dad about their latest ideas on sires for their breeding mares. Quinn listened carefully; developing Crooked Valley's bucking stock was part of his job and one he wished he was better at. When Kailey finally came out of her room, Quinn found himself wishing he had a dynamite stud in his stable. That would make all the difference in the world, but coming up with the capital to buy such an animal was a big sticking point. The ranch simply didn't have the money right now.

"You ready?" Kailey asked, grinning widely.

Quinn shook his head. "Whooeee, girl. Ain't I the lucky one."

"If I thought you meant that, I'd go put on a pair of ratty jeans," she replied while her parents laughed. She was wearing a cute denim miniskirt, cowboy boots and a red plaid fitted shirt, the whole thing highlighting her curves while still being cute and modest.

Too bad Kailey was like a sister and didn't do a damned thing for him otherwise.

"I'll be having to give a good number of boys the stink-eye tonight," he said, frowning for effect.

She laughed. "Right back atcha. Is that a new shirt?"

He shook his head. "Nope. Anyway, let's get going." He said good-night to Mr. and Mrs. Brandt and they were off to town.

"The Dollar doesn't usually have a real dance on Valentine's Day. I wonder why they're doing it this year?"

Kailey shrugged and looked out the window. "Maybe they thought it would bring in a better crowd to make it official," she suggested.

Indeed, when they got to the saloon, the parking lot was packed. "Holy cow, are you sure you want to go in here? The floor will be crowded." He'd been to the Dollar several times since Marie's death, but tonight felt different. He was…nervous. And he didn't quite know why.

"Drinks are half-price until ten. Come on, Quinn." She winked at him. "We don't have to stay that long."

"Isn't that Carrie and Duke's truck?"

She squinted. "I believe it is. See? It's going to be fun." Instead of waiting for him to open her door, she hopped out of the cab. "Let's go!" she called. "My legs are freezing here!"

He truly hadn't suspected a thing. Not until the moment he stepped inside the bar and a cheer went up. Perplexed, his gaze was drawn to a banner above the bar: *Have a Heart: Benefit for Quinn and Amber Solomon.*

His throat hurt when he swallowed and heat rose to his cheeks. Jesus. Charity? That's what tonight was about?

Duke appeared at his side. "Put away your pride for one night, Quinn," he suggested, leaning close to be heard above the din. "Your friends and neighbors are all here to give you a helping hand."

Quinn looked at his friend. "I don't know what to say." Duke smiled at him and clapped him on the back.

"You'd do the same for anyone else. Just enjoy the night, okay?"

Kailey was grinning at him broadly. Carrie came over carrying a bottle of his preferred beer.

He remembered how many people had rallied around him after Marie died, bringing food and offering to take Amber places to give her life a little joy. Gibson was like that and it was one of the reasons he loved it here. But damn, he hated that twice now he'd needed help.

His gaze shifted to the area where the pool tables were. Instead of the clack of cues and balls, the green felt held an assortment of items. He could see some sort of cellophane basket done up, a mannequin head wearing a sparkling necklace and one of Junior Ellerbee's custom saddles that generally went for a big wad of cash. What the hell?

And there was Lacey. Not at dinner, but in a bottle-green dress that brought out the red tints in her hair, a pair of supple brown cowboy boots on her feet. Lord above, but she was pretty, and as she smiled at a young cowboy looking at the jewelry, Quinn caught his breath.

Damned inconvenient. He was starting to understand his unease. Somehow he'd started to move on, hadn't he? He'd been holding on to Marie's memory for dear life, just to get through. But now something else…someone else…occupied a good deal of his thoughts. He wasn't sure if it was a good thing or a bad thing, but he knew for damned sure it was uncomfortable, and a little frightening.

"Don't just stand there like an idiot," Kailey urged, nudging his elbow. "Go mingle. Say hi. See what's up for grabs at the silent auction."

Silent auction. So that's what Lacey was doing.

He took a long swig of beer and made his way through the crowd as the guest band started a rousing rendition of "Mud on the Tires" and couples formed up on the dance floor. It took quite a while for him to reach the sheltered area of the pool tables, as he was stopped every few feet by neighbors and well-wishers. By the time he reached Lacey, he wasn't sure if he was embarrassed and humbled or warmed by the generosity of the people of Gibson—or both.

"Dinner with friends, huh?" He had to speak loudly to be heard over top of the music and laughter.

"I did have dinner with friends. With Carrie and Duke and a few other people who chipped in to help set up. Roy made sure we had lots to eat." She patted her stomach and smiled. It was no secret in town that the cook had an eye for pretty women and a penchant for big portions. It made the Dollar a popular place to grab a bite.

She looked up at him hopefully. "So? What do you think?"

He couldn't deliberately douse the spark of hope in her eyes. Not without being a total jerk. "It's a bit overwhelming," he admitted. "Wonderful, but difficult, too, you know?"

"I do know. It can be hard to accept help. Almost as hard as asking for it."

She knew something about that, didn't she? His gaze clung to hers for a few more moments and he felt that strange sense of kinship with her that kept cropping up. That is, until someone jostled him from behind, pitching him forward. Lacey reached out and caught his arms, her fingers tightening around his biceps as his chest pressed against hers.

Color stained her cheeks and she bit down on her lip…

he had the ungodly urge to pull her the rest of the way against his body and kiss her again. Which would solve absolutely nothing. Besides, they were in a crowded bar. Not exactly private.

And if they were in private? Would he act differently?

She let go of his arms and stepped back, but the shy blush was still on her face. Oh, he thought he might. Which was why it was good they were in a crowded, noisy room.

"Do you want to see what we've got for silent auction, Quinn? The items are open for bid until ten, and then we're awarding the prizes." Her eyes lit up again, and he realized that they were a different color blue than usual, darker, with a hint of green picked up from the hues of her dress.

"Sure."

She led him along the tables, pointing out a gift basket from the local salon, a weekend stay at a hotel in Great Falls, handmade silver jewelry from Joey Cartright, a silversmith right here in town. Being a ranching community, there were gift certificates from the feed store, a pair of custom boots from Lamont Leather and Western Wear, and the biggest item of all, Junior's saddle. He reached out and touched the intricate detail on the leather and once again felt humbled and unworthy.

"This is too much," he said, looking down at the current bid. It stood at fifteen hundred dollars.

"Why?" Lacey tilted her head and looked at him curiously. "Quinn, you're a big part of this community. Do you know how special that is? It's amazing how people help each other here. You've had such a rough time the last few years, but you're lucky, too. You belong here.

This is your place and your people and they want to help you because they love you."

Did that include her? Because she was here and she was helping. The thought twisted something inside him. He was so attracted to her. Liked her. And yet every time she did something nice, something special, he got angry. He had to keep telling himself to stop comparing her to Marie. That no one could take Marie's place.

And then he got angry with himself for liking her so much and knowing that he shouldn't. Wasn't it disloyal?

"Sometimes it's just hard to accept help."

She laughed. "You're preaching to the choir. Do you think I was in a big hurry to come back to the ranch when I lost my job? I had to swallow a lot of pride, you know."

Another reminder that the ranch was something she'd never wanted. If he could only remember that, perhaps he could forget about the rest. Like how tiny she looked in that dress, with the slim belt fastened at her waist. Or the way her lips were soft when they were pressed against his… God, he was getting so sick of fighting it. Wished there were fewer consequences to consider and that he could be free to just do what he wanted without having to worry about his decisions and how they'd affect everyone else. His daughter. Duke. Lacey.

Himself.

"These days," she continued on, as if oblivious to his turbulent thoughts, "I think being at Crooked Valley was meant to be. I like it more than I expected to."

"I told you." He smiled back at her politely, knowing he should feel glad she'd embraced life at the ranch. If Lacey took on her third of the ranch, they were that much closer to keeping it in the family and providing everyone with some security. Including him, and his job. Wasn't that what they'd all hoped for?

But then the flip side of that was knowing that if she did stay on, she'd be a part of his life. Perhaps on the periphery, but there, nonetheless. He'd have to get control of his feelings if that were to happen.

This wasn't even supposed to be an issue.

"I'm going to go mingle," he said, leaning forward just a little as another song started up and the noise increased. "I'll see you around."

Was that disappointment in her eyes? He rather thought it might be. But she simply gave him a little wave and turned her back on him, going to straighten one of the displays and talk to some of the ranch women who'd dragged their husbands out. He heard Lacey's bright voice ringing out over the clutter of music and conversation. "Ladies," she sang out, "you'll want to get your husbands to bid on this! Nothing says Valentine's Day like new jewelry!"

Chapter Ten

Another hour had passed and Lacey was getting tired. She looked around the room, searching for Quinn. He was holding up a corner with a couple of ranch hands from a nearby spread, watching couples spinning on the floor. About a half dozen girls sent inviting looks their way, and Lacey felt a spurt of jealousy. But while Quinn urged his companions to take advantage with nods and elbows, he didn't seem interested.

Kailey was taking a turn on the floor with one of her old beaux, Colt Black, laughing at something he said. Even though Lacey had dressed up and made a real effort tonight, she'd never felt so old and out of place. She was not even thirty, for Pete's sake. But while time hadn't made her old, life had. If not old, weary. Too weary to get very excited for the bar scene.

Now Quinn was standing alone, holding up the wall, and she made her way to his side. "Penny for your thoughts," Lacey said by his ear.

He looked over at her, his eyes shadowed. "You really want to know?"

She shrugged. "Try me."

He lifted one eyebrow. "I feel old."

She was so relieved, she started laughing. "Me, too!"

He rolled his eyes. "You? Come on."

"I dunno," she said, letting her eyes rove over the crowded dance floor. "The bar scene just isn't for me. I think I just lost the ability to be…carefree."

"You're young. Beautiful. With a lot ahead of you. You definitely shouldn't feel old."

Did he even realize what he'd just said? He'd called her young and beautiful, things she hadn't felt for a long, long time. But she wasn't about to ask him if he meant it, and open that whole can of worms. She just let the compliment sink in, let herself enjoy it for what it was.

"It's not like you're in your dotage, Quinn." She nudged his arm with her elbow. "How old are you? Thirty-five?"

"Thirty-four in June," he responded. She noticed he'd switched out his beer for a soda just as she had. She wasn't sure if they were both boring or simply cautious. Sometimes she longed to just cut loose, like she might have back in the old days. Oh, nothing too crazy, but without this looming sense of responsibility she always seemed to feel.

It was something that had absolutely nothing to do with age.

"You and I are old souls, Quinn. It's experience that's made us old, not years. And I think we've both had enough heartache for a lifetime."

He looked over at her. "You're comparing your divorce to Marie's death?"

Touchy subject, and she wasn't trying to downplay his pain, but that didn't lessen what she'd gone through. "No, of course not. Losing your wife was devastating, I'm sure. But I want you to think about something. Didn't you love each other until the end? At least you can say that. From everything I've heard, you had a beautiful relationship, one you can look back on without regrets. Me? Not so much. It's really hard to know that the person you promised to love forever—who promised to love you—chose to walk away. It's not easy to be rejected that way."

Quinn looked at her then. Really looked at her, with understanding eyes. "You loved him a lot."

"I did. I thought it would last forever. And then it didn't."

"But you get a do-over."

"And so do you. I think we both know that do-overs aren't as easy as they sound. You don't know everything about me, Quinn. Just as I'm sure I don't know everything about you. But I think we at least have that in common. Wounds can be slow to heal."

"Yes, they can," he agreed. What she didn't know was how much she was helping him heal his.

They were gazing into each other's eyes when Kailey bounced up. "Hey y'all, look who I found!"

Lacey turned her head and let out a happy squeal. "Rylan! Oh, my gosh, what are you doing here?"

Her younger brother grinned at her, picked her up and twirled her around. "Duke called me. When that didn't work, he sicced Carrie on me. I'm headed to North Dakota tomorrow, but I thought I could squeeze in a quick visit." He put her down and held his hand out to Quinn. "Sorry to hear about your place, Quinn."

Quinn shook his hand. "Thanks, Rylan."

"You should check out the auction items, Ry."

"I already did. That is a sweet saddle up for bid. Whoever made that has some serious talent."

"Junior Ellerbee," Lacey replied. "Well, then you

should catch a few dances with a few pretty girls." Lacey gave him a nudge. "Don't be like Quinn here and hold up the wall all night."

He looked over at Kailey, who'd gone to the bar in search of another drink. "I'm not sure that's such a good idea."

"It's just a dance. Quinn, you want a refill? I think I'll join Kailey."

"I'm good," he replied.

Lacey grabbed another soda for herself and a beer for Quinn anyway, because he looked like he could still use some loosening up. And she grabbed Kailey, too, and brought her back to the group. Despite what Rylan said, he'd noticed Kailey for sure. It wouldn't hurt for him to give her a turn on the floor. The vibe between the two men was a bit tense, though, so Lacey pasted on her brightest smile and beckoned for Duke and Carrie to join them. In moments, the six of them were chatting away until Cy Williamson, the saloon owner, got up to speak when the band took a break.

"Hey, everyone," he began. "Thanks for coming tonight and helping out a neighbor…Gibson's own Quinn Solomon and that gorgeous little girl of his. As you all know, Quinn's house suffered serious damage in a fire a few weeks ago. Tonight's proceeds will go right to Quinn to help him fix up his home and get life back to normal."

Cheers and claps echoed through the bar.

"And now, here are Carrie and Lacey to say a few words."

Lacey followed Carrie to the stage, and waited while Carrie said a few words about Quinn and thanked everyone for their generous donations. Kailey scooted up to hand Lacey a sheaf of papers—the bids from the silent auction. When it was her turn, she stepped up onto the low platform and took the microphone that Carrie handed her.

She scanned the sea of faces looking up at her and realized that this truly did feel like home. Like she belonged here, not just as Duke's little sister but as a part of the community. She owed a lot of that to Carrie and Kailey, who'd included her in the planning for tonight. But there was more, too. She'd made connections in town, either by running errands or shopping with Amber or looking for work. She'd had her co-workers at her last job, and her elderly neighbor, but none of them had contacted her in the weeks since she'd left Helena. The last time she'd been to the diner, however, at least three people had made a point to stop and chat and ask how things were at the ranch and with Quinn.

She really didn't want to leave. She wanted to be a part of this—permanently. It was a complete surprise, but there it was.

"Hi, everyone," she began hesitantly, her voice echoing through the mic. "I'm Lacey Duggan, Joe's granddaughter. I've got the results of the bidding right here in my hand, and some of you are going home with some wonderful items tonight. If I call your name, come to the stage at the end of the list to pay your money and pick up your prize."

She began with the gift certificates for stores around town, then moved on to the bigger items. Duke got high bid for the custom boots, while Dan Ketchum paid a ridiculous amount for the silver necklace and earrings, earning him a smacking kiss from his wife as everyone laughed.

"Now, for the saddle. I don't have to tell you all that

this is a gorgeous item worth a lot of coin. Sincere thanks to Junior for donating it tonight. Junior, I can say with complete confidence that your saddle is going to be in very good hands. The high bid, which brought a whopping three thousand three hundred dollars, goes to Rylan Duggan."

Cheers went up and Duke gave Rylan a slap on the back. Quinn looked stunned. Lacey didn't even know Rylan had that kind of money, but he knew the rules. If the winner couldn't pay up, the item went to the next best bid. Lacey withdrew to the side of the stage and the chatter built up again through the room while canned country music played until the band returned.

She collected cash and checks and crossed items off the master list until finally Rylan was the last one there. He pulled out a roll of bills and started counting off in hundreds while Lacey gaped.

"Rylan. Where did you get that kind of money?"

He looked at her blandly. "Don't worry about it."

"You shouldn't be carrying around that much cash." She frowned at him, took what he owed, and saw he still had a decent-sized roll of bills.

He looked utterly unconcerned. "I didn't have time to go to the bank earlier today, that's all."

She pursed her lips together. She hardly ever saw her younger brother, and their relationship was tenuous at best. The last thing she wanted to do was antagonize him tonight, though alarm bells were going off in her head.

But she couldn't resist saying, "You're not into anything you shouldn't be, are you?"

Familiar blue eyes looked down into hers and his lips tipped up on one side. "Don't worry about it, sis. Nothing the IRS wouldn't approve of."

Why didn't that make her feel any better?

"Can I take the saddle at the end of the night?"

"Of course."

He went to turn away but she stopped him. "Rylan?"

He looked back.

"Don't be a stranger, okay?"

He frowned and came back. "What do you mean? Are you staying on at Crooked Valley, too? Man, I can't believe Duke convinced you. You were pretty adamant at Christmas."

"I'm still working it out. And I won't be staying on the ranch, just in the area. I've offered to take over doing the bookkeeping at Crooked Valley. I've already got a few clients in town, too. Kailey's family, for one. They're bucking stock contractors, you know."

Something flashed in Rylan's eyes but it was gone as quickly as it had come.

"I'm making a run for the NFR championship this year, Lace. Don't count on me being around much. I think I've got a real shot."

So he wouldn't be looking at taking on his third. Not before the first anniversary of Granddad Joe's death, anyway. She was surprised how disappointed she felt.

"Visit when you can, then," she suggested.

Kailey's laugh drifted over the noise of the crowd. "I'll try," he said, his gaze searching out the source of the laugh. He leaned in and kissed her cheek. "Thanks, sis."

When he was gone she rested her weight on one hip and frowned. Something was going on with her brother. She just wished she knew what it was. But then, Rylan had always been the hardest of them to pin down.

By the time she'd double-counted the money and stored it in Cy's safe, the party was back to full swing.

Duke and Carrie were dancing, and so were Kailey and Rylan while Colt Black scowled at them from the sidelines. From everything Carrie said, this was a good thing. Her sister-in-law didn't seem to think very much of Colt and his on-again-off-again attention to Kailey.

Even Quinn had been dancing, with one of the waitresses that Lacey remembered from the diner. When the song changed, his popularity increased as he was snagged by Chrissy Baumgartner who worked at the library. Lacey liked her; the librarian was in her thirties, full-figured and with a smile that lit up a room. Quinn spun her around and they were both laughing and Lacey found herself grinning as she watched. It was good to see him smiling and not scowling. He was so handsome when he relaxed and had a good time.

She wished she didn't care so much.

The music thumped through the bar and Lacey leaned against a post, resting her head against the wood and enjoying the sight of so much merriment. Truth was, she cared for Quinn. She understood his pain, too. It only served to make her care more, but it was exactly the reason why nothing could happen between them again. She already knew what it felt like to be found lacking. There was no way on earth she could possibly live up to Marie's memory. It was plain to see that Quinn had practically made her into a saint in his mind.

When the song ended, she took him another beer. "Here," she offered, holding it out. "My treat."

He frowned. "I can't, Lace. Thanks though. I brought Kailey in the truck."

"I don't think you're going to have to worry about giving her a lift home," Lacey argued, nodding towards where Kailey and Rylan were talking. They only had eyes for each other.

"Is that wise?"

Lacey thought for a moment. She and Rylan weren't as close as they used to be for sure, and his money situation had definitely taken her by surprise. But she'd never known him to mistreat a woman. "They're both grown-ups. Kailey's smart and Rylan's a gentleman."

He nodded, but didn't look satisfied.

"Anyway, I can always drive your truck home if you want to have a few beers. It's no biggie if you want to cut loose a bit. When did you really get out and have fun last, Quinn?"

He shrugged. "Probably the same time you did."

He had her there. But he took the bottle from her anyway. "You're sure?"

"I'm sure. I don't mind being your wingman tonight."

"Thank you, Lacey."

"You're welcome."

"No," he contradicted, taking her hand and pulling her to the side, where it was marginally quieter. "I mean it. Thank you for everything. For your help doing this tonight, for your help with Amber, for all of it. I haven't always been fair to you. It's…complicated."

Her heart softened. "I know it is."

"I don't know how to do this." He looked over the crowd, took a long pull off the bottle, then looked at her again. "Do you know what I'm saying?"

Her heart started to beat a little faster. "I think I do."

"You see, I let myself get close, and then I get scared and then I push you away and I'm mean about it. It's not your fault." His gorgeous eyes delved into hers. "I've held onto my grief for so long, it's like an old friend. I don't know what to do without it, you know?"

Oh, mercy. Her pulse was fairly hammering now. Maybe it was the alcohol or the fact that the crowd and noise provided a measure of protection, but he was being all honest again.

"I do know. It's how you protect yourself from being vulnerable."

"And then I feel guilty when I...when we..."

He didn't finish the sentences, but it just took gazing into his eyes to understand the rest of the words. This would be so much easier if she didn't find him so irresistible...

She tried being flippant to lighten the mood. "Hey, are you admitting you like me, Quinn?" She sent him a dazzling smile.

But he didn't smile in return, just took her hand in his and squeezed her fingers. "More than is good for either of us, Lacey. And I'll be damned if I know what to do about it."

They stood there, in a little bubble of intimacy, oblivious to the people milling about. She squeezed his fingers back. "You could always ask me to dance."

A ghost of a smile flirted with his lips. "Miss Duggan, may I have this dance?" He rubbed his thumb along the side of her hand and a shot of pure electricity zipped up her arm.

"Of course," she answered. After all, what could happen on a crowded dance floor? It had to be safer than being cozied up here in the corner.

Quinn put his bottle on a nearby table and led her to the floor. Just as they arrived, the current song ended and they waited for the next one. When the opening measures began, Lacey began to laugh. "Oh, my. Are you up for this?"

The singer was doing a respectable imitation of Alan Jackson's voice in "I Don't Even Know Your Name" and couples paired up for a polka.

"Are you kidding? I was born doing a polka."

"Your poor mother."

He raised his arms in the correct posture. "Chicken?"

She laughed at the impish look on his face. He was so easy to like when he let go of the chip on his shoulder. "Not even a little bit." She stepped up and put her hand in his and her other on his shoulder. Before she could even catch a breath, he whirled her into the dance.

He was smooth. And he knew how to lead, too, sweeping her into the steps with surprising ease. It had been a long time since she'd danced like this and she felt a little rusty, but once they'd negotiated the floor in a full circle, she started to relax and get into the rhythm a little more. Quinn could tell, too, because he guided her into a spin that stole her breath and would have had her laughing if she hadn't had to shift into the steps right away.

She looked into his face and saw him grinning from ear to ear, his eyes twinkling at her as he spun her in a turn so quick she wasn't sure her feet even touched the floor. They were good together, dammit. So good that she just stopped thinking and threw herself into the dance with a carefree abandon she'd forgotten she possessed.

When the song ended, they were both winded and laughing and clapping for the band, and Lacey noticed that several faces were turned towards them and smiling. "That was so fun!" she exclaimed, pressing her hand to her chest. "Oh, my gosh. I haven't danced like that in years! Who knew you had it in you, Solomon?"

Whether it was the beer or the dance talking, she didn't know, but she got a little thrill when he winked at her and said, "You haven't seen all my moves yet."

Lord help her, she wanted to. They'd been doing this on-again-off-again thing for weeks now. She suspected it was because they both tended to overthink. To over-feel. It was hard to do that when you were galloping across a dance floor.

The next song was a line dance and Lacey laughed and pulled her hair up into a ponytail to help cool her neck. Quinn waggled his eyebrows as everyone lined up for a tush push and the band launched right into the fast-paced "Trouble." The steps were quick and light and Lacey was treated to a fabulous view of Quinn's back-side as he wiggled it from side to side midway through the sequence. There were whoops and hollers from the crowd and clapping from the sidelines as the lines of dancers stomped their way through the song. When had she last had this much fun? When had she allowed her-self to cut loose and just enjoy something? She pivoted, did the three-step and clapped, and laughed from the sheer joy of it. Quinn looked over and grinned at her and she felt a strange sensation that in this moment, right now, she was exactly where she was meant to be.

With a final stomp the dance was over and the singer took a quick few moments to grab his water bottle. Quinn took Lacey's hand and led her from the floor straight to the bar, where they both ordered a water to help cool them down.

"Oh, Quinn! That was so fun. You're a great dancer."

"I haven't done that since..." His face clouded, but

only for a moment. "Never mind how long. Thank you, Lacey."

"Anytime. I'm a bit rusty but funny how it all comes back to you."

"Tell me about it." His gaze met hers and she wondered what else they were rusty at—and if it would come back just as quickly as the dance steps.

She shouldn't be thinking that way.

The next song was a waltz. As soon as the opening bars started, Carrie and Duke, Kailey and Rylan, and most of the other couples moved to the crowded floor. Lacey looked at them with longing, but honestly the dance area was so jammed full of couples there wasn't much room to dance properly.

"Popular dance on Valentine's Day," he said, not looking at her.

"Seems like it."

He was quiet for a few seconds and then he asked, "Do you have a coat? I could use a cooldown. The water didn't quite cut it."

Butterflies began to flutter in her stomach. "I do. It's in the office."

"You want to get some fresh air?"

She nodded, feeling words strangle in her throat. "I'll just be a second."

The office was quieter, the sounds muffled through the thick walls, and Lacey took a moment to breathe deeply and consider what she was doing. Maybe it was all innocent. Maybe Quinn really did just want to cool off.

Maybe it was something more.

Or maybe she just wanted it to be.

Chapter Eleven

The air was crisp and cool outside the Silver Dollar, and Quinn and Lacey weren't the only ones to go outside. A few other couples left and a handful were outside taking a smoke break and chatting. Quinn took Lacey's hand in his and led her away from the entrance, around to the side of the log building, where it was quieter and more private.

At this point she didn't need to dance; her stomach was doing enough of a jig all on its own.

He let go of her fingers and put his hands in the pockets of his jacket, lifting his face to the sky. "It's a nice night. Not too cold. Clear."

Indeed, the sky was inky black, with the pinpoint dots of the stars winking down on them.

"In the city, sometimes the streetlights affect the visibility. I love the sky out here. It goes on forever." She let out a contented sigh.

"You hated it when you first arrived."

"I didn't hate it." She looked over at him. "I resented it. Big difference."

He smiled a little. "You don't like to be told what to do, do you?"

She smiled back. "What was your first clue?" She

gazed up at the constellations. "It isn't just being told what to do. It's feeling like, I don't know, like I'm being shoehorned into something. Like I don't have a choice."

"You have choices, Lacey. Lots and lots of choices."

Didn't she just. And one was figuring out how exactly to proceed with the man beside her. Did she want to risk it? Or just back off? She'd probably get hurt in the end. There could never be anything serious between them, anyway. He'd made that abundantly clear.

"Does this mean we're going to stop fighting now, Quinn? It gets exhausting, treading on eggshells around you."

"I'd like to stop fighting. You make it difficult."

"I don't mean to be bitchy…"

"Not that, Lacey. That's not what I meant."

He put his hands on her shoulders and turned her to face him. The door to the bar closed and all was silent in the parking lot, except for the muffled sound of the second waltz in the set. His face loomed above hers, shadowed in the darkness away from the lights of the entrance, and she could see the little puffs of his breath in the air.

She rather thought he might kiss her, but instead he slid his hand down her arm to clasp her fingers and put his other hand at the small of her back, drawing her close.

Oh, Lord. Quinn Solomon was a romantic. He had to be, because he was dancing with her in slow, narrow steps, beneath a winter moon.

It was impossible not to get caught up in the moment. She noticed everything about him—the way he smelled, how his cologne was magnified by the heat of his body after the fast dances, the roughness of his palm as it pressed against hers, the size of his body as it moved against her smaller one. With a little jolt of surprise, she realized that he'd put on weight over the past few weeks, lost that gaunt, lean look she'd noticed when he'd first arrived. A little sliver of female satisfaction warmed her, as she wondered if it was due to her home cooking. Maybe Quinn was right after all. She was a nurturer at heart. Liked to take care of people. Liked to take care of him.

She was treading into dangerous territory.

They were so close now that their coats were pressed together and his jaw grazed her temple, a stubbled caress that fuelled the fire of her desire for him. If their first kiss was anything to go by, Quinn had a lot of passion inside. Wrong or right, wise or foolish, she wanted to be the one to unleash it. She lifted her chin just a little, rubbing against him, a little nudge of invitation.

He nudged back, a silent acknowledgment, acceptance, and they embarked on a dance of anticipation so sweet that she held her breath, waiting for the moment when he'd finally give in and kiss her.

The tip of his nose was cold but his lips were warm when they finally descended on hers. Their feet stopped moving to the music, and Lacey lifted her arms, wrapping them around his neck to hold him close.

He did his part in that regard, his strong hand pressing on the curve of her bottom, an impassioned sound rippling up from his throat and sliding through her like an aphrodisiac.

Quinn, she thought. *Oh, Quinn.*

He put his other arm around her and lifted her up as if she weighed nothing at all, then walked forward until they were up against the rough logs of the saloon.

With the wall behind her, he was able to press against her body and have his hands free. He put them on either side of her face and kissed her again and again until her knees went weak and she nearly forgot where they were.

The door to the saloon slammed and Lacey realized that things had gotten a little out of control when their bodies froze. It had been more than kissing—it was full-on making out. Quinn had been rubbing against her rhythmically, one hand had undone the buttons of her coat and he was cupping her breast through the thin fabric of her dress.

Thankfully Quinn shifted so that his body sheltered her from the view of the people leaving the bar.

"Jeez, get a room," one of them jeered, laughing, and she looked up at him. His eyes were nearly black in the darkness, but there was something else there, too. Agreement.

They had a whole big house to themselves tonight. All it would take was a ten-minute drive and they'd be free to do whatever they wanted.

She gulped, wanting it so badly she ached. She was terrified, too.

"It's up to you," he murmured, running one finger down her cheek in a soft caress. "I don't want to stop here. But I understand if you do…"

"You're sure?" she asked, her words a breathy sigh.

"You drive me crazy," he replied. "So damn crazy, Lace. You have for weeks. I gotta do something about that or I'm going to explode."

Nothing he might have said would have been better for her female ego than that. A saucy grin tilted her lips as she took the leap. "Me, too. I don't want to think. I don't want to worry. I just want to touch you, Quinn.

Really touch you without wondering if we're going to get caught."

He chuckled, a sexy, soft sound. "Darlin', getting caught is half the fun, don't you know that?"

"Take me home, Quinn."

With one last searing look, he backed away, grabbed her hand, and led her to his truck.

BECAUSE HE'D BEEN a little free with the beer, he handed Lacey the keys. It didn't seem super romantic or manly, but he hadn't abandoned all sense. She'd just adjusted the seat and started the engine when he spied another couple preparing to leave: Kailey and Rylan. Rylan was putting the saddle in the back and Kailey was hopping into the cab. As Lacey put the truck in gear, Quinn's phone buzzed.

I don't need a drive. You have a good night.

Kailey must have noticed their disappearance, but he found he didn't really care. Everything he did had been catalogued by this town. Just this once he wanted to do something impulsive and crazy without the worry of how it looked or what was appropriate. Didn't he deserve that? Hadn't he been through enough? For one night, he wanted to know what it was to live again rather than just go through the motions.

"Text message?" Lacey asked, turning on the blinker for the main road.

"Kailey. She left with your brother."

She spared him a quick glance and then put her attention back on the road. "It's Valentine's Day, Quinn. Romance is in the air."

"So it is."

"She's a big girl."

"Yep."

"Quinn?"

"What?"

"Why does this drive seem so long?"

The simple question had him questioning his sanity, because it made him want to pull the truck over to the side of the road and end the wait to take her in his arms. He clenched his fingers into fists.

The drive seemed to take forever and yet, somehow, only a few minutes and they were back at the house. There was a moment of hesitation when she cut the engine and they sat in the silence. Maybe she'd changed her mind. Maybe he should. He didn't want to give her false hope for the future. He couldn't honestly think beyond tonight. Beyond this moment.

But his thoughts were interrupted by Lacey, sliding across the seat, running her hand through his hair. That was all it took for him to pick up exactly where they'd left off, pressed up against the cold side of the Silver Dollar. His mouth fused to hers as he pulled her into his lap, the feel of her body warm against his.

"Let's get inside," he suggested, taking a precious moment away from her lips. Blindly, he undid his seat belt and opened the door, then miraculously got them both out of the vehicle without too much fumbling. Quinn slammed the door and then picked Lacey up in his arms, heading for the house with long, purposeful strides.

"Quinn," she whispered against his neck, and the soft awe he heard in her voice made him feel about ten feet tall. He'd never been one for big romantic gestures, but damn, it had been a long dry spell.

Unlocking the door proved slightly tricky, but within moments they were in the foyer. Quinn put her down on the stair steps and knelt before her to take off her boots, his hand sliding down the smooth expanse of her calf. He removed his own footwear, slid off his jacket, took her coat and finally, finally met her gaze.

Her eyes glowed with heat and longing and his body responded. He hadn't wanted a woman like this in months. Not since...no. Dammit, he wouldn't think of that tonight. Tonight, the weight of the past would stay in the past. There was a beautiful woman in front of him, as eager for him as he was for her. He reached behind her and pulled the elastic from her hair, freeing the ponytail so that the copper waves fell about her shoulders. God, he loved her hair.

"Lacey." Her name was a low rumble in the quiet, dark house. "Are you sure?"

She stood up, standing on the bottom step, which put them eye to eye. Her hand rested against the side of his face. "All the times we argued and fought...that's passion, Quinn. I don't want to fight it anymore. I want to put it to better use. I want you to make love to me."

He took her upstairs to her room, to the master bedroom with its four-poster and thick mattress and soft-as-feathers duvet. Gazes locked, they undressed each other, no shyness, no false modesty. She was so beautiful, all creamy skin and slender limbs and that glorious mane of hair. When he took off his shirt, her fingers grazed his abdomen. "Oh," she said, biting down on her lip. Knowing she approved only fired his desire further.

They took their time, touching, kissing, caressing, until he couldn't wait any longer. "Do we need to take precautions?" he asked, hoping to God she was on the pill because he hadn't bought a condom in years.

Her startled gaze clashed with his, and then slid away. "No," she replied softly. "I'm good."

"Good?" Something didn't feel quite right about her response. He didn't want to kill the mood but he needed to be sure, too. He wanted to protect her. Protect both of them.

"I'm safe," she answered. "No worries there, Quinn. I promise."

Lacey was a lot of things, but she wasn't a liar and she wasn't manipulative. If she said they were safe, he trusted her.

As the February moon shone through the window, he let his gaze travel down the length of her lissome body once more. Then he closed his eyes and made her his, losing himself completely to pleasure.

VALENTINE'S DAY.

Lacey lay perfectly still in the bed, staring at the ceiling as dawn slowly broke. Beside her, Quinn lay on his side, his back to her, his breathing deep and even.

She had slept with her roommate, with the one man who drove her absolutely bananas, on Valentine's Day, that horrible, wonderful day that happened each year and made people crazy. This was a real first. And now she was wondering how to proceed. Should she try to extricate herself from the bed quietly, without waking him? She was stark naked under the soft sheets, but her robe was hanging on the back of the bathroom door. If she could reach it, she could at least cover herself…

Or should she stay? Wait for Quinn to wake up, leave first? She turned her head carefully, trying to be per-

fectly silent. Half of his back was visible above the edge
of the sheet, and she gazed at his strong, broad shoulders, slightly freckled skin and a small scar that left a
puckered pink mark right in between his shoulder blades.
His hair was mussed, pushed to one side, but lying flat
in the back.

A man in her bed. The first man since Carter. And
Carter had been the only man since she was twenty.

She was hardly prolific in the sexual partners area.
That wasn't a bad thing, but it did make last night perhaps slightly more important than it might have been if
she tended to be more, well, casual about things.

He shifted slightly and she froze, but he settled
once more, his breathing deep and rhythmic. His body
warmed the bed, and her eyes drifted closed again, soak-
ing in the moment. The truth was, she knew Quinn was
unavailable. No matter what had happened last night,
she knew for him it had just been about sex. Scratching an itch.

Hadn't it?

Carefully, she rolled to her left side, her body curl-
ing into the same position as his, but inches away so
she wasn't technically spooning him. She wished she
could. Wished she could curl up behind him, wrap her
arm around his waist and rest her cheek against his back,
drawing on his warmth and strength.

He'd been a wonderful lover. Attentive, intense, making sure she got her share of pleasure…and she had.
More than once. It was funny how arousal took over,
plunging them into the moment, where they'd been
able to be utterly naked—not just with their bodies, but
with their needs and feelings. Completely devoid of false
modesty and lacking in self-consciousness.

There'd been a moment when he'd looked down into her eyes that she'd felt something click. Something she'd never expected to feel again. Tears stung her eyes now as she remembered how things had slowed down, how they'd savored each other. It hadn't been the rush of frantic sex.

It had been the slow burn of making love, just as she'd asked. But what Quinn didn't know was that they weren't just words to her. She really had made love to him, because she'd gone ahead and fallen *in* love with him.

Her throat tightened as she stared at the back of the man she wanted but knew she couldn't have. Her heart and pride had taken a beating after Carter left, but Quinn's had been utterly shattered with Marie's death. She was pretty sure he hadn't put it back together again, no matter what had happened between them last night. And the reason she knew was because he still wore his wedding ring. For some reason, it made her feel like she'd slept with another woman's husband. Maybe because, even though Marie was gone, Quinn still wasn't totally free.

Knowing she might never have another chance, she slid closer to him, until she was spooning him for real. Once he woke up, the spell would be broken. But even if it was for a few seconds, she wanted to know how it felt. She slid her arm carefully over his hips, curled against his warm body and rested her temple against his shoulder blade, breathing deeply to imprint the scent of him on her brain.

He sighed.

She closed her eyes.

It was several seconds later that he spoke. "Good morning."

"Hey," she answered. She felt exposed, naked beneath the bedding, but she was glad she hadn't sneaked away, too. These might be the last intimate moments they shared. Even if he thought they might pursue something, she knew that would change if he found out the truth.

"Some Valentine's Day, huh?"

She smiled against the soft skin of his back. "Beats a box of chocolates from the drugstore."

He chuckled, the movement brushing his body against hers in strategic places.

"Are you okay?"

He was trying to take care of her. Just like he had last night, even when there'd been no need.

"I'm fine, Quinn." More than fine.

He rolled over until he was facing her. There was morning stubble on his face, and she saw what her mom had always called "sleepy tears" in the inside corner of one of his eyes. But he was beautiful. He always had been. The difference was, she'd resented him for it before, especially when he found fault with her.

He'd certainly sung her praises last night, and she felt heat creep up her cheeks at the recollection.

"We should probably talk," he said quietly.

"I know." But then he was silent. After an uncomfortable pause, she suggested, "Do you want to go first?"

His gaze met hers, but she couldn't read what he was thinking. Not this time. "I should get up and get started on the chores first. Otherwise the boys'll be knocking on the door wondering what happened to me. That'd be awkward."

More awkward than this moment? Probably, she admitted to herself. No one needed to know what had happened here last night.

"Whatever you want," she said, trying to smile.

"Okay." He leaned closer and kissed the tip of her nose, and then moved away as if leaving the bed. But then he rolled back, braced up on an elbow.

"Lacey? Last night, when you said you were safe…"

Oh, God.

"…I just want to be sure you're okay."

It was a bit late to be sure now that the deed was done. "I'm positive," she replied, hoping he'd let the matter go. The last thing she wanted to do this morning was drop the bombshell that she couldn't ever have children. It was painful…and premature.

He smiled again. "Okay. I'll see you later?"

She nodded.

He slipped from the bed and padded—buck naked—to the bedroom door, scooting across the hall to his own room to get dressed for the day.

Lacey rolled to her back and stared at the ceiling. What on earth were they going to do now? They couldn't dance around each other forever, it would only make things tense.

The conversation she didn't want to have was inevitable…and necessary. There was no sense in being in denial about anything, because it only masked a truth that would eventually come to light.

Truth was, she'd let herself fall. For Amber, for Crooked Valley, for the damned town…and for Quinn Solomon most of all.

Chapter Twelve

Lacey was able to put off the conversation for several hours. She had a shower, tidied her bedroom and caught a ride into town with Carrie so they could get the proceeds from the benefit from the Silver Dollar safe and deposit it at the bank. Cy had graciously tallied up the entire amount complete with one of his deposit forms so all they had to do was pick it up. Lacey goggled at the total at the bottom. All told, the benefit had raised nearly ten thousand dollars for Quinn and Amber.

Carrie had a doctor's appointment, so Lacey offered to take it to the bank herself. Carrie stopped her at the door to the saloon as they were leaving, putting a hand on her arm.

"Lacey, are you okay today?"

Lacey looked up at her sister-in-law and friend, and saw real concern marring her normally happy face. "Of course I am."

"You're real quiet this morning."

"Just tired after all the excitement of the last few days." She smiled reassuringly. She hoped.

"You left your car here last night."

"Quinn had been drinking. I offered to drive him home."

"In his truck, not your car."

It was starting to feel a bit like an inquisition.

"I guess I thought he might need his truck this morning. For, uh, ranch stuff."

Carrie's eyes were a little too sharp for Lacey's liking. "How bad is it?"

"What?" She opened her car door and threw the deposit bag on the passenger seat.

"You can't kid a kidder, sweetie. I went through plenty of pains when I fell for your brother. Lots of doubt and indecision."

"Who said anyone's falling for...anyone?" Cripes, one mention of Quinn and she couldn't even form a proper sentence.

"So it's just sex? You're not in love with him?"

Lacey choked on her own spit and started to cough. "Jeez, Carrie. Blunt much?"

Carrie laughed a little before her face turned dead serious again. "Look, I saw you two dancing last night. I've seen the way you light up when you're together. The way sparks fly off when you argue. It's...familiar. I just don't want to see either of you get hurt."

"Me, either," Lacey admitted.

"And there's Amber to think of."

Lacey thought of Amber asking if she'd be her mommy and her stomach twisted.

"I didn't even say we slept together." She was rather proud how definitively that came out of her mouth.

"Oh honey, you didn't have to." Carrie looked at her with sympathy softening her features. "*Are* you in love with him?"

Lacey heaved out a sigh. "I don't know. And we need to talk, but I'm scared."

"He doesn't know?"

Carrie didn't have to elaborate; Lacey understood her meaning. "No. When I said he didn't need protection, he accepted it at face value." Her shoulders slumped. "God, he's really trusting, isn't he?"

"That's the thing, Lace. He's usually not. But he trusts you. That's a good sign, right?"

"Sure. Until I tell him the truth. Of course, he might be spending today trying to find a way to let me down gently. Maybe I should just tell him and let him off the hook."

"You think he won't be interested if he knows you can't have kids?"

She didn't answer, which she figured was answer enough.

"Do you want to be with him?"

"I don't know. I care for him. A lot. Enough that maybe the kindest thing would be to let him go. That way he can find someone he deserves. Someone who can give Amber a brother or sister. Maybe one of each. He's such a good dad and she's a great kid. They deserve that..."

"What a load of horse crap." Carrie made a disgusted sound.

"Carrie, I know you're happy with Duke and everything, but sometimes it's not that easy."

Carrie laughed out loud. "You think we were easy? Oh, my gosh. That's funny." She took Lacey's hands in hers and squeezed before letting them go. "Here's the thing. You went through hell, and the person who was supposed to be with you through it all bailed. Now you don't believe anyone will be there for you. But at some point you have to have a little faith, you know?"

What she was saying made sense. In theory. "I'm afraid my faith is in short supply."

Carrie frowned. "Well, don't give up. That's all I'm saying. Quinn might surprise you."

"Quinn's still in love with Marie."

"Is he? Or does he just think he is because he thinks he should be?"

All the questions were giving Lacey a headache. "Listen, Dr. Ruth, I've got to get to the bank and deposit this cash. And you need to get to your appointment and make sure that baby is doing okay. You can psychoanalyze both of us later."

Carrie responded with a lopsided smile. "I know. Duke told me not to interfere. I couldn't help myself."

This time it was Lacey who put her hand on Carrie's arm. "And I appreciate the thought. Just let us work it out ourselves, okay?"

"Okay."

Impulsively Carrie gave Lacey a hug. "You know, I always wanted a sister. Sorry if I get carried away and go overboard."

She'd let go and was heading to her old truck when she turned back around. "At least tell me one thing. Was it good?"

Lacey burst out laughing at the expectant look on Carrie's face. "That's for me to know and you to ponder," she called back, then got into her car. Despite the meddling, she suspected she'd like having a sister of her own, too. Duke had chosen exceptionally well.

Lacey worked herself up to talking to Quinn when she returned home, but his truck was gone and she found a note saying he'd gone to pick up Amber at his mother's. Restless, Lacey did a load of laundry and cleaned the upstairs bathrooms just to keep busy. She started the makings of a beef stew, letting the meat simmer with garlic and thyme and some red wine, then poured a small glass for herself that she sipped while making baking powder biscuits. Anything to keep busy and not think too much about what she was going to say when they were finally alone again. Maybe it would be best to just let Quinn guide her. She'd gauge the situation as they went along.

It was going on five when the truck finally pulled into the yard again. Amber came barreling inside, straight to the kitchen, dropping her overnight backpack on the floor as she rushed to tell Lacey all about the previous day's party, the Valentine's cards from her classmates, and her night at Grandma's.

"Whoa, slow down, kiddo! Where's your dad?"

"He said he was going to look after the chores and then he'd be in for dinner. I'm hungry."

Lacey laughed, but her heart gave a bittersweet pang. The more Amber chattered, the more Lacey was sure she had to tell Quinn the truth. It wouldn't be fair to really start something with him and keep her situation a secret.

The pan of biscuits came out of the oven and she put them on a rack to cool. Then she eyed the wine bottle again. She might need a bit more liquid courage to get through the hours ahead.

Quinn came in and washed up for dinner; Amber kept up sufficient chatter about her Valentine's Day party and her sleepover that Lacey and Quinn were spared having to make much conversation. After dinner, Lacey cleaned up while Quinn took Amber upstairs for her bath and to read stories. By eight o'clock, Lacey was fit to be tied, knowing the conversation was coming and unsure how it would go. Amber was overtired, too, and Lacey could hear a bit of a fuss going on upstairs as Quinn attempted to settle her in bed.

When he finally came downstairs, he looked exhausted. Maybe they should table talking until there was a better time…

"Wow," he said quietly, coming into the kitchen. "She was full of beans tonight."

"It sounds like she had an exciting time. And she's overstimulated and tired all at once."

"I know. I gotta say, though, when she starts with the whiny stuff, my patience dwindles pretty quickly."

Lacey chuckled and tucked some plastic dishes under the cupboard.

"Lacey, about last night…"

Here it comes, she thought. She schooled her face into a polite mask, a light smile with what she hoped was an "it's all good" expression.

"Now that Amber's home, it's probably not a good idea to…you know. Have a repeat."

Right. Discretion and all that. She didn't know whether to feel relieved or disappointed.

"Of course. The last thing she needs is more confusion and upset. After what she said the other night…"

"I'm just not sure that being…open with this is in her best interests right now. You're really important to her. To us. I just think we need to be careful, you know?"

Wait, what? Was he actually thinking of pursuing something with her? "Careful?"

He nodded. Met her gaze evenly, and the attraction to him spun through her core unbidden. All he had to do was look at her like there was nothing else around and she was a goner.

"Things were hard for Duke and Carrie. I know they're happy now, but she got pregnant so fast. It was really hard for them at first. I'm not sure what I want, Lacey. Until I know, until we know..."

She turned away, got down another wineglass, and poured a few ounces of ruby-red liquid in the bottom.

"Lacey?"

She gulped down the wine. In her heart she knew it wouldn't make this any easier, but she had to do something. Her hand shook as she put down the glass, the base of it clanking a little too loudly on the countertop.

"I told you, Quinn, you don't have to worry about that." Breathe, she reminded herself. Long, calming breaths.

"I know. But no method is a hundred percent."

She could do this. She had to do this. It was only fair to everyone for her to have full disclosure. "Well, there are a few methods that are."

She could have sworn she saw disappointment darken his gaze. "You mean abstinence. You really think last night was a mistake, then?"

"No!" She replied before she could even consider another response. "Quinn, no. Unless...unless you do."

Here she went again. Afraid to voice her own feelings, wants, needs. She'd gotten so used to holding things back, to calculating what to say to keep things from getting worse. She'd done it all the time when she and Carter were struggling, just to keep from having another argument. She was aware that she did it, but not sure how to stop.

"Let's go sit down," he suggested.

They went to the sofa and she perched on the edge, like a bird on a branch ready to flee at any moment. This was crazy. She was in love with him. Shouldn't she be throwing her arms around him, ready to explore what might evolve between them? Why couldn't she allow herself to be happy?

"Lacey," he said softly, covering her hand with his own. "What's wrong?"

She looked down at their joined hands. Willed the right words to come. Never in a million years had she imagined herself in this position. Not even after that crazy kiss in his office. This was different. Real. Terrifying.

Sad.

And that was it, wasn't it? She was sad. Sad that circumstances were what they were. Sad that nothing could be changed. She'd made peace with it long ago, but that didn't stop her from feeling like garbage about it.

"I didn't expect this," she began, staring at her knees. "We were always bickering. Finding fault with each other. And then I got to know you better."

"I got to know you, too." His voice was warm and affectionate.

"But you don't really know me, Quinn." She looked up at him. "That's just it. You know the parts that I've let you know."

"I know your divorce had a profound effect on you. That it's been hard for you to bounce back from that rejection."

Bless him, he was trying. After being such a curmudgeon when they first met, the effort for tenderness and understanding only underscored how wonderful a man he was. "Oh, if it were only that." She sighed. "Honestly, Quinn, it's what led up to the divorce that really did a number on me. You had a brilliant marriage with

Marie. I know that. A fool can see it. I can't begin to compete with that."

His hand slid from hers. "I won't deny that. We were really happy, and she was a wonderful wife and mom."

Lacey's heart sank even further.

"But Lacey, I never expected to feel like this again. Happy. Looking to the future, because I had something worth looking forward to. Something changed for me last night, do you get that? I took the first steps in moving on. I'm trying very hard not to feel guilty about it, or like I'm somehow betraying Marie's memory because the truth is she's gone and never coming back and I'm still here."

His gaze held hers. "Look, I'm definitely not ready to move fast. I don't think anyone could be more surprised than I am, but I'm not ready to walk away from us, either."

Oh, God. He was really making it tough. That he'd started to move beyond his grief…that it was because of her only added to her burden. She didn't want to be responsible for that. "I only wanted to help the both of you out."

"Are you saying you don't have feelings for me?"

She looked deeply into his eyes, wished she could say she didn't. It would all end right here. Clean break, move on. Could she lie that convincingly? But Quinn never gave her the opportunity.

"I was there last night," he murmured. "With you. Inside you. I don't think you're that good of an actress, Lacey Duggan."

She swallowed. "I have feelings, okay? I couldn't have been with you last night without them."

"So what? We were ships passing in the night?" The

words were harder now, with an edge of hurt underlining them.

"I can't give you what you want, Quinn. I'm sorry."

Silence fell over the room, awkward and heavy.

After a few moments he spoke again. "What if what I want is you?"

The weight of the words pressed against her heart. "You are just realizing that there is a life out there waiting for you," she replied, her stomach a tangle of anxiety. "You're a family man—everyone can see that. You need a woman who can be the wife and mother you need. Don't you want brothers and sisters for Amber?"

"Maybe someday, but that's putting the cart a little ahead of the horse, don't you think?"

She shook her head, prayed briefly for strength and calm. "No, I don't. Because Quinn, I can never give you that. What I didn't tell you is that…that I can't have children."

She'd shocked him, that much was clear. His lips dropped open but no sound came out; his eyes widened with surprise. "So you see," she continued, "as much as last night was wonderful, I can't let you believe it was something it wasn't."

"Wow." His shoulders slumped a little as he let out a big breath. "I wasn't expecting that."

"I'm sorry, Quinn. Maybe I should have stopped things before they got…intimate. You were just kissing me and it felt so good and it had been so long since I felt that desirable. Wanted." She blinked, looked down. "That makes me sound opportunistic and a little vain."

"If you are, so am I."

She looked back up at him.

"Hey," he said softly. "You're not the only one who was suffering a crisis of virility."

"You carried me across the yard and…"

He grinned, a fleeting flash of teeth that reminded her of why she liked him so much. "And your face when I took my shirt off fed my ego."

Damn. They weren't supposed to be playing into the sexual tension here.

But the mood turned serious again. "Lacey, there are treatments you can try. I don't want to see you close a door prematurely. You'd be a wonderful mother."

Tears stung the backs of her eyes. "Thanks for the compliment, but I've been down that road, Quinn. I tried treatments and procedures. I had scarring from endometriosis. At first it was just the pain and I was on meds for that, but then when we kept trying to get pregnant, and nothing happened, I went on hormone treatment. In the end I had a hysterectomy. No amount of treatment can help me now, you see. I can't carry a child without a uterus."

There. It was out.

"When you mentioned about the birth control then… wow, you really meant it."

She nodded. "You need to understand that we married young. We had high hopes and plans for this great future. You know the type. A house and a yard and a few kids running around with the family dog. But there were no kids. No dog. I held on to that dream too tightly. Carter was a bit of a jackass for leaving, but I can't say he shoulders all the blame. My whole life became about hormones and fertility, I used up our savings and we didn't even have the joy of a great sex life to keep us going because I had so much pain. By the time I had the hysterectomy, the marriage was beyond repair. My last bit of false hope was gone. The last thing I want to do, Quinn, is give you that hope and then disappoint you in the end. You've been through enough."

She raised her hand and put it on his cheek. "I care about you too much. I probably should have been honest before, but we were arguing and then I thought the whole attraction thing was one-sided. It's not something I'm particularly open about."

"I'm so, so sorry," he answered, putting his hand over top of hers. "And to have Amber here, and Carrie pregnant next door...that must be so hard for you."

She shook her head, more touched than she cared to admit by his consideration. "Carrie and Duke know, and I would never begrudge my brother his happiness. At first it was a challenge, I admit. It was better after I told them."

"They knew."

"Yes."

Was he mad about being left out of the sharing circle? She half wished he would be. It might be easier than dealing with sympathetic Quinn.

"I'm glad someone was there for you to talk to," he said. "Carrie's good at that. So's Kailey. They both listened to me often enough after Marie died."

She felt her heart clutch a little. "You have so much to offer, Quinn. You're a great dad and a good man."

"You do, too, you know."

"I'm not sure of that. My head tells me I'm still Lacey Duggan, that I still have...gumption in here somewhere." She pressed a fist to her chest. "My heart, though, isn't convinced. Logically I can tell myself that the surgery didn't make me less of a woman. But deep down, I feel like it does. And no one can change that."

Sometimes love was knowing when to let go. Lacey figured this was that moment.

His expression darkened. "Did Carter tell you that?"

He had. Not all the time, but when he got particularly frustrated. Lacey had felt like such a failure as a woman. Before the surgery, she'd been poked and prodded so many times it was ridiculous. There'd been hormonal swings and side effects, and sex had become mechanical. Even then, she'd held herself stiff, bracing for the pain that usually happened when they made love. She had felt totally and utterly betrayed by her body. When Carter had said he was done pretending, it had been a relief.

"I thought we would start over after the surgery. Get some counseling to put our marriage back together. Instead he moved out and started divorce proceedings right away. And he stuck me with the debt that we'd accumulated through all the treatments. You want to know why I had no emergency fund when I lost my job? I'm still paying those bills."

"He didn't help pay?"

"I was the one who pushed, so I was the one to pay."

To her surprise, he slid over on the sofa cushion until his thigh was pressed against hers, and he put his arm around her shoulders, urging her to lean on him. She didn't want to, but he was so warm and strong and she was feeling so drained from this whole truth thing that she wilted a bit, resting her head on his shoulder.

"Honey, I think you've already paid enough."

She wouldn't cry. She wouldn't.

But she was very, very close.

She turned into his embrace and let him hold her, let

his steadfast strength give her a little bolster against all the hurt and disappointments. This was the problem with Quinn. If he were just a lover, it would be easier. But he was a friend, too. Sometimes they fought, sometimes they annoyed each other, but when the chips were down, he was the kind of man she could count on. Never before had she wished so fervently that she could be more perfect. Less flawed.

She sniffed.

He rubbed her back and said nothing, which was exactly what she needed.

When it had gone on long enough, she pushed her way out of his arms again. "Thank you," she whispered. "I needed that."

"I know." He smiled at her. "So. Where do we go from here?"

She frowned. "Nowhere, I guess. I'm sorry, Quinn. I just think this is better than really hurting each other down the road. There's Amber to think of, too. I think we need to be really consistent there. She's been through enough, and I know she's already attached."

"Lots of thinking on your part."

"It's nothing you haven't already said. Besides, it's better this way."

"Better for who?"

Don't make this more difficult than it already is, she thought. "For everyone. You'll see. We should…just go on being friends. Besides, before long your house will be ready for you to move back home. Maybe this just happened because we spend so much time together already. We've been playing house, you know? But it's not reality."

It sounded good. Even if she didn't quite believe it herself.

"If that's what you want." He sounded resigned and she tried to regret being with him last night. Tried because while she knew it would have been smarter, she couldn't quite bring herself to feel sorry for how amazing it had been to feel that cherished and loved once again.

"I think it's best."

He put his hands on his knees, pushed himself to standing. "I guess I'd better get some shut-eye, then. Lots to catch up on tomorrow."

He was about to pass her on his way to the hall, but he stopped and knelt before her, putting his hands on her knees, his face just below hers so she couldn't avoid looking into his eyes.

"You have so much to offer, Lacey. Don't let anyone tell you differently. You got that?"

She was in danger of sniffing again, but was saved when he got up and walked away. His footsteps sounded in muffled beats on the stairs, and still she sat there, not quite sure what to do with herself. Water ran in the upstairs bathroom, the toilet flushed, and the floors creaked a little as he went to his room and shut the door.

She had to get up, move, go to bed. Tomorrow was another day.

It was all fine until she went to crawl into bed. When she snuggled into the bedding, the scent of him wafted up from the sheets, an olfactory memory that immediately transported her to the previous night. A longing she wasn't prepared for pierced her heart, stealing her breath, until the tears she'd held back so valiantly in the living room came trickling down her cheeks.

All she'd ever wanted was a normal life. Nothing

fancy. The love of a good man, a home to call her own, a family to love and care for. But she could never give Quinn the babies he wanted. The only thing worse than this feeling right now was knowing that she'd let down another man she loved.

Chapter Thirteen

Quinn saddled up Big Turk, one of the geldings, and went for a long ride. He needed to get out of the house and into the sunshine. Amber was at a playdate with one of her classmates, whose parents would bring her home in time for dinner. Right now what Quinn needed most was wide-open space, fresh air and some perspective.

Turk was raring to go, dancing a little bit as Quinn held him back on the way to the east side of the ranch. There'd be time to let him loose once they got over the ridge and onto the flat part of the pasture. The sun was warm on Quinn's back, a harbinger of the milder spring temperatures to come. Soon the melt would start, calves would be born, the grass would green and sure, they'd have a few more snowstorms. They always did. But the hardest part of the winter was nearly over.

They hit the flats and Quinn gave Turk a nudge, both of them enjoying the run. It cleared away the cobwebs.

His mind kept going around and around, thinking about what Lacey had said. She'd raised a lot of questions about how he saw his future. A couple of months ago he would have said bringing up Amber in the house where she'd been born, and working at Crooked Valley, helping Duke make the place profitable again. Something had changed since Christmas. And that change was Lacey. Suddenly he wanted more.

Turk was getting lathered, so he slowed to a trot for a few minutes and then back to a walk again, heading to the top of a butte overlooking a creek bed. They crested the rise and Quinn took a deep, cleansing breath. Acres and acres of rolling pastureland spread out before him, the wide-open space awe-inspiring. Limitless.

He frowned a little. That's what Lacey had brought to his life. A sense of limitlessness, that there was more out there for him than his myopic vision. She had made him ask questions of himself, like what he really wanted out of his life. Before Lacey, he hadn't considered other children, but now…she was right. He wanted them. He wanted Amber to know brothers and sisters. He wanted a home with warmth and laughter and not just getting by. Lacey had given him that over the last weeks, bringing him back to life bit by bit. He'd let things go the other night because he'd known two things: he needed to think about what she was saying, and she'd made up her mind and nothing would change it, at least at that time.

The big question was, what was he going to do about it now? There was no escaping the fact that Lacey couldn't give him those children. But the home with warmth and laughter? Someone to share his life with, to talk to at the end of the day? He could see all those things with her. He had put all of his energy into his daughter, but even he could see the difference in the dynamic when Lacey was around. There was an ease to things when Lacey was added to the equation. A sense of rightness that had been missing when he and Amber had been muddling through.

Maybe, just maybe, if he could convince her to give

them a try, they could look at other options for building their family.

Good heavens, was he really thinking about a future? Marriage? It seemed premature, and yet, in his situation, he didn't really know how to do casual. Any woman he dated—and Lacey was the first—had to be viewed as a potential mom for Amber. That's just how it was when you were a single parent. It was a package deal. His heart gave a little thump when he realized that Lacey and Amber had gotten along awesomely from the beginning. She was kind and firm and fun, and his daughter, who had once been insecure, had started to blossom just from being around her. If only Lacey could see the miracle she'd accomplished!

Quinn turned Turk around and headed back towards home. He was facing the wind now, and he turned his collar up against the chill. The plain truth was that despite fighting it at every turn, he'd fallen in love with her. Valentine's Day hadn't been about scratching an itch. It had been about starting a new chapter of his life—a chapter with her in it.

What Lacey needed was someone to counteract all the cruddy hogwash that Carter had fed her. The whole thing about him deserving better and her being less of a woman was bull. It wasn't like it was her choice to be sick. He'd like five minutes alone with her ex-husband to set him straight. But seeing as that wasn't likely and probably wouldn't help matters anyway, he figured that he needed to find a way to help her rebuild that confidence the way she'd rebuilt his. To let her see that she could have those things. That she deserved them.

It wasn't until he was nearly to the barnyard again that he came up with an idea. He'd need Amber's help, of course, but that wouldn't be a problem. His daughter would love this particular job.

He took a half hour to settle Turk and then he headed to his office to make some phone calls.

QUINN PULLED IN to the driveway and looked over at Amber. She was practically bouncing in her seat, anxious to get out and see the puppies.

"Okay, so you need to remember that this puppy is for Lacey, right?" He wanted Amber to be part of it, but wanted her to be prepared for the fact that the dog would be living at Crooked Valley and not at their house. He didn't expect it would be too rough because Amber spent a lot of time at the ranch and could see Lacey's dog often.

"I know, Daddy, I know. Come *on*!" She struggled impatiently with the seat belt crossing her booster seat. With a laugh, Quinn reached back and helped and she was out of the truck in a jiffy.

Sue Bramstock had a litter of puppies for sale and Quinn had remembered Lacey talking about planning the house, kids, picket fence and dogs. Well, she had the house, if she wanted to keep it. The Crooked Valley big house suited her to a tee. Instead of picket fences, there were corrals and pastures, and Quinn couldn't do anything about the kids. But he could get her a dog.

He took Amber's hand and they made their way to the house. It took longer than he expected, because Amber got sidetracked by the chicken coop and fence, and had to go watch the hens peck around with their necks jutting back and forth. The rooster crowed and she giggled as she stood on the bottom rung and peered over the top. "Why don't we have chickens, Daddy?"

He'd never considered it. "I don't know."

"We should have chickens. They're funny."

One hen came over and looked them over with a beady eye, her head tilted to one side as if to say "What are you lookin' at?" Amber giggled.

The Bramstocks were the kind of farmers who were self-sufficient. They made their living with beef, but they also kept chickens, a few hogs and had a giant vegetable garden in the summer. He remembered years ago when Eileen Duggan had kept a huge garden. Joe had never found the time or the motivation to keep it up after she died.

"Come on, munchkin. Let's see the puppies."

"Okay." She took his hand again and hopped off the fence, and they went up the stairs to the front door and knocked.

Sue answered the door with an apron covering her jeans and sweatshirt. "Quinn! Good to see you. Come on in."

It smelled like apple pie in the house and his stomach growled. But he was soon distracted by a series of yips and shrill barks.

Sue grinned. "I've got the pups in the mudroom while I bake. There are four of them, about fourteen weeks old, and mature enough they are getting in my hair and under my feet. If you want to scoot over to the side door, I'll meet you there."

Quinn and Amber did indeed scoot. The ground was soft from the mild weather and the snow mixed with mud under their feet. Quinn got Amber to stomp hers off as best she could before they stepped inside the mudroom where Sue's husband, John, left his outerwear and boots.

"Oh!" Amber squealed at her first glimpse of the puppies, which were bigger than Quinn had expected. She dropped to her knees, utterly fearless, and was immediately mauled by brown-and-black bundles of fur, complete with pink tongues ready to kiss their new admirer.

He couldn't help but laugh.

"They're a little excitable yet," Sue said. "But house-training has been going pretty well. They're smart dogs."

"You said they're a shepherd/retriever cross?"

"That's right. So they'll be a good size, but a really nice temperament. I love them." Sue reached down and gave the mama a pat. "Xena here is so loving, but when a stranger comes in, her guard dog tendencies take over. I like that. I feel safe, but she's not an aggressive dog. Know what I mean?"

"I do." And he liked the idea of Lacey having a protector, especially when he wasn't there anymore and she was in the house alone.

"Daddy, this one likes me!"

Three of the puppies were roughhousing in the middle of the floor, but a fourth was climbing into Amber's lap. His fur was a dark tan color, with black markings around his eyes, ears and feet. "He's a handsome boy, that's for sure," Quinn agreed.

Amber hugged him close and he certainly didn't seem to mind. "He's funny. And his paws are huge!"

"He'll grow into them," Quinn answered, knowing that they wouldn't be puppies for long. Already they'd lost the little-ball-of-fur look to them.

Another one jumped up on Amber's lap, kissing her face. "Can we get two, Daddy? Please?"

Oh, no. Quinn shook his head. "Remember. Just one today…"

"For Lacey. I know." Her face fell a little. "But I love

this one, too. And she is his sister. Sisters and brothers should be together, shouldn't they?"

It was hard to argue with that. "Honey, we can't have two puppies at the ranch."

"Why not?"

He was scrambling for an answer when she was distracted with playing again and he was saved. He looked over at Sue, who was watching him with an amused expression. "I know," he said, sighing. "I have a hard time saying no."

"She's a good kid, Quinn. And I understand how hard it is. I think it's got to be even worse when you're a single parent."

He nodded. "Look, our house should be ready in a few weeks. Any chance of you holding the girl until then?" He kept his voice low, so as not to give Amber any false hopes.

"I can probably do that."

"Just don't let on to Amber. We're still staying at Crooked Valley while the repairs are being done. She'll get her puppy fix there for a while. Probably more than she realizes."

"No problem." Sue and Quinn went over details like what dog food she was using and how much, if he had a crate and leash and all the other things he'd need. The crate he'd borrowed from Kailey's family, who kept a couple of border collies. The leash and collar he'd bought in town at the department store, along with a couple of ceramic dog bowls.

He took along the little bit of paperwork from the vet so they had a record of vaccinations, and the recommended age for neutering. Amber crawled out from beneath the mob, begging for the honor of sitting with the puppy on the drive home.

In very little time, they were back out in the truck, the puppy secured in the crate on the front seat, which Quinn had pushed all the way back. Amber was pouting, but when they got to Crooked Valley he clipped on the leash and let Amber take the pup for a quick pee before introducing him to Lacey.

He was suddenly nervous. He picked up the puppy and carried him to the front door, then opened it, because since that first morning the door had been unlocked during the day. He was hoping to tell Lacey himself, but Amber raced ahead, muddy boots and all, crying out "Lacey! Lacey! We gots you a puppy!"

Lacey came around the corner, tugged by an excited four-year-old. Her eyes got huge as she saw Quinn with the puppy in his arms. "You really did. Holy shit."

Amber halted abruptly. "You said a bad word."

Lacey's cheeks flamed. "Sorry."

She was immediately forgiven and Amber smiled again. "We got you a puppy, Lacey! Isn't he cute?"

Still she didn't say anything, and Quinn felt a sense of unease slide through his body. Maybe this hadn't been the smartest move. "Amber, can you go to the truck and get the bag of stuff?"

"Okay, Daddy!" She opened the door and then looked back at Lacey. "Wait'll you see the dog bowls me 'n' Daddy picked out."

She slammed out of the foyer.

"Quinn?"

He swallowed. Hard. "He's a shepherd/retriever cross. Three and a half months old, partially house-trained and guaranteed to be a sweetheart."

Tentatively she reached out and touched the soft fur. The pup wriggled excitedly, so Quinn put him down on the floor but kept him on the leash.

"Why would you do this? A dog?"

He stood up again, met her gaze. "You gave up everything. You said it yourself…the house, the kids, the dog and the picket fence. But you don't have to, Lacey. This can be your home, you see? The fences are here…maybe not the picket ones you imagined, but they're your legacy. And the dog…he'll be great company for you. You've lost enough. I just wanted to give something back to you."

To his relief, tears gathered in the corners of her eyes. "Well." She laughed, emotion filling her voice. "You are a man of surprises, Quinn Solomon. That's a lovely thought. Truly." The pup pulled on the leash and gave a sharp bark. "But a puppy?"

"If you really don't want him, I guess I could take him back to Sue's." Or his house. He was pretty sure Amber wouldn't mind, but he was still disappointed that his gesture wasn't welcome.

"Oh, it's not a case of wanting! He's awfully cute." She smiled hesitantly. "I just…I've never had a puppy before. I have no idea what I'm doing."

"Never?" Relief rushed through him. Was that all?

She shook her head. "I always wanted one, but Mom was afraid of dogs."

"Well, this one's yours if you want him."

They shared a long look, and then Lacey sat down on the stairs. As soon as she did, the puppy rushed over and started to climb up on her.

She gathered him up on her lap, started to laugh when he began licking her face…and then got a strange look of horror.

Amber rushed back in with the shopping bag.

"Um…we're going to need some paper towel," Lacey suggested, putting the dog on the floor again. "And I need new pants."

"Eeeew!" Amber wrinkled her nose. "Bad puppy!"

Lacey laughed. "Aw, he was just excited. Puppies pee a lot. If he's going to stay here, you're going to have to keep your eye out for puddle accidents."

"Yuck!" Amber suddenly seemed disenchanted.

"He's a baby," Lacey explained. "Do you remember when you had to be potty trained?"

Amber nodded, though Quinn wondered if she actually did remember such a thing. "Well, doggies have to be house-trained so that they go to the bathroom outside. I might need your help with that."

"You need me to help?"

Lacey was winning over his daughter like a champ, not that she needed to try hard. It was so clear to him now. There was a reason she'd come here. And that, as far as he could tell, was to put a little sunshine back into his life. He wanted to be able to do that for her, too.

"Sometimes. Especially if I'm busy. And puppies have a lot of energy. He might need some playtime with toys, so he doesn't chew things."

"I can play with him!"

"Well, phew. That's a load off my mind, kiddo." She laughed. "But first, could you grab the roll of paper towel?"

Amber rushed away.

"You have a real way with her," he said, down low.

"Kids are people, too. They like to feel needed and important. As far as the dog, I don't know if I want to thank you or strangle you." The pup was sitting pretty as you please now, still on the leash. "But he *is* awfully cute."

Quinn stepped forward, ignoring the pull of the leash. "Lacey, you deserve to be happy. Stop punishing yourself."

"Quinn, if you did this to change my mind…"

Had he? He didn't think so. Though perhaps he had, just a little. Not to blackmail her, of course not. He wasn't into trying to buy someone's affections. But if he could make her see that the kid thing didn't matter…

"I did it because I didn't think you'd do it for yourself. And because a dog can be a great companion."

"Because I'll never have my own kids."

Frustrated, he heaved out a breath. "That's not what I said."

"Here you go, Lacey!" Amber came back with the towels, ripped off a few sheets and handed them over.

"Thank you, sweetie." Lacey wiped up the little puddle on the stairs. "I'll be right back. I need to change into some sweats or something."

She disappeared up the stairs, while Quinn waited at the bottom, not sure how to handle her latest accusation. All he'd wanted to do was give her something she'd always wanted. To see her smile.

Why did women always have to invent motives for everything?

Chapter Fourteen

Lacey's hands trembled as she pulled the sweats out of her dresser drawer. A puppy! Of all the romantic gestures she might have expected, this was the last thing she would have thought of. But there he'd been, standing in the doorway with the most adorable puppy she'd ever seen cuddled in his arms.

She was scared to death. Puppies were a lot of work! She didn't have to have owned one before to know that. But she was also incredibly touched. It was only the knowledge that Quinn wanted more kids that held her back from falling into his arms. The temptation was there, but in the end she knew the truth would come out, just as it had with Carter. They'd pretend it didn't matter until they couldn't pretend any longer. She wasn't sure she could stand to watch another man she loved walk away.

She peeled off her jeans and hung them over the shower rod to dry and pulled on the soft sweatpants. They'd have to get the dog settled and then think about dinner. It would serve to take her mind off her latest failure: she'd been told she'd hear by today about the job she'd interviewed for last week. The phone had been silent, so she assumed that the position had been given to someone else.

Back downstairs, there was a clanging sound coming from the living room. Quinn was assembling a wire dog crate, and Amber was dancing around with the dishes in her hands, wondering where would be the best place for "puppy" to eat.

Lord help her, it felt like a real family.

THE ENCHANTMENT WITH the "real" family evaporated quickly. Amber didn't want to go to bed before the dog, but wanted to stay up until they decided on a name. Quinn put his foot down, which resulted in the tears and wails of an uncharacteristic tantrum. Lacey's ears were still ringing when she took the pup outside for what felt like the tenth time. At bedtime, she put him in his crate in the living room, but she wasn't in bed five minutes when she heard him whining and crying. Quinn heard it too, and suggested that the puppy might need company. There was no way she was sleeping on the sofa, so Quinn took the dog, crate and all, and moved it to her bedroom.

She was nearly asleep when the whining started again. Lacey was half-tempted to let him out of the crate and on the bed, but she didn't want to get into that habit. Finally, she turned on the radio on her phone that was plugged into the dock, and set the volume low. That, at least, calmed the puppy.

At four in the morning the whining was more of a yelp. She pushed on her slippers and clomped downstairs with him, reaching for the leash on the hook by the door and letting him outside. Aggravated, she stared at Quinn's closed door with a fair bit of hostility. The reality of puppies was very different than the idea of all that cuteness.

She'd gone back to sleep, but when Quinn got up at six-thirty, she stuck her head under a pillow to blot out the sound of the shower. Pup heard the noise and started bouncing around in the crate. Where on earth did he get all the energy?

She didn't let him out of the crate until she'd had a quick shower and had pulled on a pair of comfortable jeans and an oversized hoodie. Once more, she trotted outdoors with him on the leash, then came back in just as Amber was coming down the stairs.

"Can I feed him? Please?"

"Sure. Be my guest." Amber could feed the dog while Lacey made much-needed coffee.

"Come on, dog." Amber sent Lacey a disapproving look. "He needs a name."

"I'll decide on one today, I promise."

"I can help." She set her chin defiantly.

Lacey hesitated. It was as plain as the nose on her face that Amber was already in love with the dog. That she was feeling proprietary. Had Quinn truly thought this through? What would happen when they moved back to their house and the dog stayed here? Could she really do that to Amber? In her head she knew it probably wasn't smart to give in because she felt sorry for the little girl. But her heart…how could she let Amber start to get attached and then break them up?

Quinn came down the stairs and took one look at her before veering off to the side.

"Rough night?" he asked, his voice innocently calm.

"You could say that."

"Aw, he just needs to adjust. He probably missed the other dogs last night. New place and all that."

"Great." She took a sip of her fresh coffee and closed her eyes for a moment. Amber was chatting away to the dog as she put a scoop of food in the bowl. "Quinn," she said quietly, "what happens when you move back home? She's going to hate to leave him."

"We talked about it. She knows she can see him whenever she's here."

"You think that's going to be enough?"

He frowned. "Don't worry about Amber. Anyway, we need to stop calling him 'dog' and 'puppy.' You come up with a name yet?"

She had, though she felt kind of silly about it. "When I was a kid, I read this book that I loved. There was a dog in it, and he was always getting into scrapes but helping people out. I know, it sounds lame, but he was great. His name was Ranger."

Quinn laughed. "I think I remember that book. The dog was even a shepherd, if memory serves."

"He was." She felt a little sheepish. Really, a kid's book? But there it was. "I always thought if I got a dog, I'd call him Ranger."

"You're sentimental," he observed, a grin tugging at his cheek. "Who'da thunk it?"

"Smart-ass," she murmured.

"What do you think, Amber? Lacey's going to name him Ranger."

Amber wrinkled her nose. "I like George."

Quinn caught Lacey's eye, then looked at Amber. "Well, Lacey gets to do the honors because Ranger is her dog, right?"

"I guess." Amber looked so crestfallen that Lacey couldn't help but offer a compromise.

"What if his middle name is George? You have a middle name, don't you?"

Amber nodded. "Amber Marie. After my mama."

It was impossible for Lacey to remain emotionally immune to the situation. "So what if we called him… Ranger George Duggan? What do you think?"

Amber giggled. "That's a long name for a dog."

"He's an important dog."

"Can I take him outside?"

Quinn looked at Lacey for permission, which she gave. "Okay," he agreed. "But on his leash, and only for fifteen minutes. When I call you to come in, you need to come in. You have to get ready for school."

"Yes, Daddy." She patted her leg. "Come on, Ranger!"

Lacey was sure that the pup had no idea that he was supposed to answer to that name, but he sure found chasing after Amber entertaining.

When the door slammed, Lacey was relieved for the reprieve from commotion. Quinn poured his coffee and smiled at her. "So," he said softly, "am I on the naughty list this morning? I know he was up in the night."

She thought for a moment but shook her head. "No. I know I'm going to love him, Quinn. Hey, if I'd had kids, I'd be up in the night, right?"

She asked it brightly but Quinn frowned. "Lacey, I've been thinking. Is there really no way? I mean—" his cheeks turned ruddy. "You uh, still have your ovaries, right? Have you considered a surrogate?"

She wished he wouldn't push for alternatives that no longer mattered. Did he honestly think she hadn't thought about these things?

"Do you know how much that costs?" She ran her hand through her hair, her fingers catching in the tangles. "There are the regular fees, legal fees, payments to the mom each month…we're talking thousands and thousands of dollars. I'm still paying off the bills from before. We didn't have that kind of money and I certainly don't now."

"I had no idea."

"I do. Believe me, I looked at all the angles."

"Adoption?"

She turned away, opened the dishwasher and began unloading it just to have something to do. "By the time we got to that part, Carter had had enough. I'm not sure he would have gone for it anyway. Not his flesh and blood, you see. And it can take years to get a baby."

"I see."

"You do?"

"Uh-huh."

She straightened and met his gaze. "And what exactly do you see?"

"I see you've given up. Truth is, I can bring home a puppy, I can tell you that you deserve happiness and I can say or do a hundred different things, but none of it is going to change your mind if you aren't open to changing it."

Her chest started to cramp. "Quinn, you know you want children."

"I have a daughter. Would I like more? Of course. But if it didn't happen? Shit, Lacey. A month ago I was sure that I'd never fall in love again, and now I have and what's standing in my way isn't grief or guilt or my feelings but your stubbornness!"

Had he really said he'd fallen in love? With her?

"It's been too fast. You don't know what you're saying."

"Let me know what the proper amount of time is to fall for someone. You know I wasn't looking. You know I went out of my way to be aggravating."

"You're still aggravating."

He stepped forward, grabbed her upper arms, and kissed her.

When she got over the initial surprise, she knew she should push him away. This wasn't helping at all. Instead she felt herself soften, lean into the kiss, open her lips beneath his. It felt so right, so perfect. The last thing she trusted was anything that seemed perfect, though, so she indulged in one last kiss before stepping back and out of his arms.

"What are you trying to prove?" she accused softly.

"That this is real. How we feel is real. And that I want to try."

Her heart hurt, both from longing and from the inevitable pain she knew was coming. "I can't, Quinn. I've been down this road before. I know you mean what you say right now. Eventually, though…"

"You won't even give us a chance."

"I'm sorry. I've been through this before and I care about you, Quinn. I'm not sure I could go through it a second time, and I would fully expect to."

He just gaped at her. The word *coward* raced through her mind but she shoved it away. She wasn't a coward. She'd simply learned her lesson, learned not to idealize situations and saw them for what they were.

"That's a real no, then."

She smiled weakly, but there was little warmth in

it. "Were you really trying to soften me up with the puppy?"

He took a step back. "I was hoping you would see that you didn't have to give up. I guess I didn't realize you already had. I should have known. I'd given up for a long time, too."

And would he again? She hated that she might cause him pain. That for the first time since his wife's death, he'd cared about someone, about her, and she was turning him away.

Better now than later, that little voice inside her whispered.

But she said nothing.

Quinn's face flattened as he shuttered away any more emotion. "Crews are working on the house this week. You'll only have to put up with us for a little while longer and then we'll be out of your hair."

She swallowed, hurt at his withdrawal, knowing she had no right to be. "There's no rush to leave, Quinn. You know you're welcome here. You have as much...no, more right to this house than I do." Her lip quivered and she bit down to stop it. "I can always stay with Duke and Carrie for a few weeks if me being here bothers you. If it's too awkward."

"I doubt you want to take Ranger there. It was a stupid idea, wasn't it? I can see if Sue will take him back."

A dull ache penetrated her stomach. "No, don't. I want to keep him. If that's okay with you."

"Fine. I'd better get Amber in to get ready for school."

Conversation over.

He was halfway down the hall when she called after him. "Quinn?"

He didn't answer.

"I'm sorry," she whispered, knowing he probably couldn't hear her, full of regret.

IT TOOK TEN days for Quinn's house to be ready to move back in. Lacey stayed out of his way as much as possible, and he stayed out of hers. They stayed civil so that Amber wouldn't notice anything was wrong, but she kept herself busy with some of her accounting jobs, looking after Ranger and visiting with Carrie a lot in the evenings.

She took phone calls intended for Quinn about the delivery of new furniture to replace that which had been damaged in the fire. New sofa, love seat, new beds for both him and Amber. It was almost March when he broke it to Amber that they would be moving back home the following day.

"Yay!" Amber cried out, her spoon clattering to the table, splattering pudding on the tablecloth.

For all her "will you be my mom" talk, Amber seemed to personify the sentiment that there really was no place like home. She seemed excited that she would be back among her familiar things—whatever had been salvaged from the smoke damage.

After dinner, Quinn disappeared with Amber to pack. Lacey cleaned up the kitchen and felt a sorrow open up inside her at the thought of being alone in the house.

Then again, she wouldn't really be alone. Quinn would be back to venturing in and out, as the ranch office was still in the house. But Amber would be gone, too. And the sensation of going to bed at night and not feeling so all alone.

She looked over at Ranger, who was curled up in a ball on the leather sofa. She hadn't had the heart to make him stay off the furniture, especially since there was no fabric upholstery. She went over and sat beside him, pleased when he unfurled his warm body and stretched, and then rested his chin on her lap. She stroked the soft fur and found her throat clogging with tears. Maybe this was why Quinn had brought Ranger home. Because he knew they were leaving and he wanted her to have some company.

He really hadn't had any faith in her. It stung that he'd been right about it, too.

The next morning Lacey got up early to make a final breakfast for Amber. Her favorite was chocolate chip pancakes, so Lacey mixed up the batter and started frying them off while bacon snapped and sizzled in another pan. Amber came skidding into the kitchen with an excited grin. "You made pancakes?"

"I sure did. Do you want to find the syrup?"

Together they set the table, while Lacey tried to ignore the sound of Quinn going in and out, taking their bags to his truck. She'd hated the fact that he was moving in and now she hated to see him go. Yes, even though they'd reached an impasse lately, the house would seem unbearably empty without him and Amber here.

His spot at the table would be vacant.

She wouldn't smell his soap and aftershave in the bathroom anymore.

Instead of off-tune whistling, there'd be nothing but silence.

She grabbed the spatula and flipped the pancakes on the griddle as Quinn came in to grab a quick breakfast before hitting the road.

"I'm going to miss Ranger," Amber said a few minutes later, her mouth stuffed full of pancake.

"And I'm going to miss your help." Not exactly, but she would never tell Amber that. Sometimes kid and dog made more mess than they solved, but she wouldn't have traded it for anything. "You can come back to see him anytime, though. Have playdates!"

Amber giggled. "That's funny. Puppy playdates."

"We'd better get going," Quinn said firmly, putting his knife and fork on his plate and taking a last swig of coffee. "Thanks for breakfast this morning, Lacey."

Ouch. So impersonal. In such a rush to leave... "You're welcome. It's the least I could do."

He refused to meet her eyes. Amber collected her plate and, like the angel she was, started to take it to the dishwasher.

"Just leave it, I'll clean up. Your daddy's in a rush." A rush to get away from her. Either he was still really angry about what had happened, or she'd truly hurt him. She didn't like either option very much.

Amber took a minute to stop and hug Ranger, who was sitting beside Lacey's chair, hoping for a scrap of something to fall to the floor. "'Bye, Ranger. See you soon. Be a good doggie."

"What about me?" Lacey asked. "Do I get a hug?"

"O'course!" exclaimed Amber, barreling forward and wrapping her arms around Lacey's neck as Lacey leaned down. "I love you, Lacey." As if that weren't enough, Amber placed a sweet, smacking kiss on Lacey's cheek.

Quinn was right. Get out and get out fast, preferably before she embarrassed herself. For a moment, her gaze lifted and met Quinn's. There was no escaping the pain in his eyes. He wasn't leaving unscathed, either. But it was for the best. Wasn't it?

"Come on, Amber. Gotta get you to school and then unload the boxes."

"Coming, Daddy!"

She raced off to put on her boots and jacket, and Lacey followed, despondency leaching into her body, making it feel heavy and sluggish. She loved him. She truly did. She loved his strength and kindness and ethics and honesty. She loved watching him play with Amber, or help her with her letters, or any of the other things that required patience and love since he'd taken on this single-parenting gig. And it was for that reason alone that she let him go. Someone out there would make him happy, give him more children to spoil. Give Amber the opportunity to have brothers and sisters.

Amber ran to the truck and Quinn got her fastened in, then came back to the door for one last duffle bag.

It was in his hand before he looked up at her, standing by the banister.

"Well, this is it," he said, his voice betraying no emotion. "Thank you, Lacey, for sharing your space with us. You must be glad to be getting the house to yourself again."

Really? Did he actually just say that? It made her a little bit mad that he could reduce what had happened here the last month to her wanting her space back. "That's it?" Her tone was brittle. "That's all these last weeks have been? Like you're checking out of a hotel?"

The crests of his cheeks pinked. "Don't make this harder than it already is."

"Then don't pretend that it's something it's not." She huffed out a breath. "Or rather that it's nothing when it was something."

Anger flashed in his eyes. "You refuse to let it be

something. So it's just better this way. We can go back to me working in the office when I need to and if that's a problem I can talk to Duke about putting an office in the horse barn. There's room."

"You're punishing me."

He shook his head. "No, Lacey, I'm trying not to punish myself. Big difference."

Before she could reply, he nodded. "Gotta go. Amber's waiting. Thanks for everything."

He turned and walked away.

She stared after him until Ranger noticed the open door and made a run for it. The sound of his claws on the floor alerted her and she neatly stepped aside, blocking his path. Then she shut the door.

Chapter Fifteen

It was as if someone had taken all the color out of her life.

There were no little pink-and-purple piles of clothing to be picked up, hardly any dirty dishes and no more coffee breaks at the kitchen table. What had initially been peace and quiet and order was now dull and silent and lonely. Ranger kept her busy and she clung on to caring for him like a lifeline, taking him for long walks around the ranch, enjoying the fresh air now that spring was around the corner. He started chewing her slippers, so she made a trip to the pet store for some better chew toys to keep him occupied. In the evenings, he often hopped up on the sofa with her as she watched TV. There was just one problem. Every time she looked at him she saw Quinn, standing in the doorway with a hopeful look on his face, Ranger in his arms.

For the millionth time, she wished things were different. She wished they could just have a normal life with the normal progression of things: fall in love, get married, have children. No bumps in the road, no…

She sighed, put her hand on Ranger's warm coat. No sacrifices or gut-wrenching decisions. Why did life have to be so complicated?

A week passed, then another. Lacey worked on the

ranch books, then hung out her shingle for doing taxes as the season was in full swing. It kept her busy most days, papers spread out on the kitchen table. When she had a lull, she drove over to the Brandt spread to catch up with the monthly accounting.

Once more she was struck by the prosperous state of the ranch. It was so put together, so tidy and cared for. If she could do anything for Crooked Valley, she hoped it was find ways to save Duke some money so he could afford to make the little upgrades and give the place some polish. She'd discovered that the bucking stock side of the operation wasn't carrying its weight, and she wanted to speak to Duke about some options for either making it profitable or shedding themselves of the liability. Maybe talking to Kailey would help, too. The girl knew her business.

"Hey, girlfriend." Right on cue, Kailey stuck her head inside the office. "Saw your car out front and brought you some coffee."

Lacey let out a breath and smiled. "Thanks. I could use another cup."

"Not sleeping well? You look tired." She put the mug on the desk.

Lacey raised an eyebrow. "Gee, thanks for the compliment. Actually, the dog keeps me up a lot of nights. Though he's getting better."

"He's a cutie. I saw him when I was over to see Quinn a few days ago about one of the mares."

"You didn't come in?"

"Your car was gone," Kailey explained. "You know, you'd think Quinn would be happy, being back in his own place again. But a sorrier sight I've never seen. He's practically moping around."

Kailey's voice was a little too innocent, her gaze a little too knowing. Lacey took a sip of her coffee. "Don't start," she warned.

"Come on." Kailey sat across the desk from Lacey and rested her elbows on the scarred wood. "What happened with you two? Valentine's Day you couldn't keep your eyes off each other, and I bet that extended to your hands, too."

Lacey's cheeks heated.

"See? I'm right. We all figured things were headed in a new direction and honestly, I was really happy about it. He's not the kind of guy who should be alone forever. He's too wonderful."

Yes, it was well established that Quinn was practically a saint. "Then you marry him," Lacey snapped.

Kailey sat back. "Whoa. First of all, Quinn and I are friends. Always have been. Kissing him would be like kissing my brother. Yuck." She frowned at Lacey. "Second, what the hell is with the marriage thing? Did he ask you? Oh, my God. He did, didn't he?"

"No, he didn't," Lacey replied. "Thank God."

Kailey scowled. "Girl, what's wrong with you? Quinn's an amazing guy. And you know it, so what gives?"

Lacey deliberated for a moment. Truth was, other than Carrie, Kailey was her only other real friend here in Gibson. "It's just better this way," she hedged.

"Better? Better how? And Amber...she loves you. All she talked about was helping you cook and Lacey this and Lacey that..."

Pain sliced through Lacey's heart. It wasn't just Quinn she missed, it was Amber, too.

"I can't have children, Kailey." She closed her eyes and just let out the words.

She heard Kailey blow out a breath. When Lacey opened her eyes, Kailey was looking at her with sympathy softening her gaze.

"I'm sorry, Lace. I shouldn't have pushed. I had no idea."

"It's not something I talk about," she admitted. "I told Carrie and Duke a while ago. I told Quinn after Valentine's Day."

Kailey wasn't stupid. She put things together quickly. "When things got to a point where he needed to know."

"Yes." She gave a small nod.

"Oh, honey."

"Don't." Lacey held up a hand, determined not to get weepy. She proceeded to fill Kailey in on the painful details of her condition. "It is what it is. So now you see why Quinn and I can't be together."

Kailey's brows pulled together. "No, I don't. Not really."

"Quinn wants more kids. I could see it, and I called him on it. It's no sense pretending it doesn't matter. We'd just be fooling ourselves and then one day we wouldn't be able to ignore it any longer."

"Like you and your ex?"

Lacey looked into Kailey's eyes. "Yeah. Like that."

There was a moment of quiet while Kailey considered her next words. But if Lacey was expecting understanding or sympathy, she was way off base.

"So you're just giving up?" Kailey sat back in her chair, her lips pursed. "Do you know how hard it had to have been for Quinn to even care about someone again? What he's been through?"

"Of course I know!" Lacey bit down on her lip. "You don't think I've thought about it every day? How losing

Marie destroyed his life and how incredible it is that he cares for me? You don't think this hurts?"

"Then fight for it. If you love him, why can't you fight for him?"

"Because I can't stand to think of the look in his eyes when he tells me he can't do it anymore. Just thinking about it makes this giant hole open up inside me, Kailey."

"And what makes you so sure he will?" Kailey leaned forward, pressing.

Lacey didn't know what to say. She was afraid, pure and simple. Afraid of letting Quinn down. Afraid that everything Carter had said to her the day he left would be true. That if she hadn't fought so hard, maybe she wouldn't have strangled their marriage to death.

"Kailey," she said softly, painfully. "I fought for this for years. I did treatments, surgeries, you name it. I fought for the family I couldn't have and in the end I drove my husband away. I made him hate me."

It was a few seconds before Kailey answered, but then she reached over and touched Lacey's hand. "Honey, have you considered that you fought for the family, but you forgot to fight for him?"

She took some time to think about that. Had she been so obsessed with a baby that she'd forgotten about her husband? What if he hadn't cared about it as much as she had? She'd been so worried about the status of her uterus that she'd forgotten to consider the status of her relationship with Carter.

She knew how to fight. But what if she'd just been fighting for the wrong things?

Kailey cleared her throat. "Sweetie, isn't Quinn worth fighting for? If he's not, then it's better this way. But if he is…what the hell are you doing sitting here?"

"I can't give him babies," Lacey reminded her, a catch in her voice.

"He has Amber. It's not like you're telling him he'll never be a father, and even if it was, don't you think that when you love someone, you love all of them? Not just the good stuff. What you have to decide is if you trust in him, if you believe in him enough to fight for the two of you. He's not Carter. You can't judge all men by the one man who let you down." Something passed over her face, something Lacey thought looked like pain but it quickly disappeared. Kailey pressed on. "At some point you have to have a little faith."

The idea was scary enough that Lacey's chest started to tighten and it was hard to breathe. She knew how to fight hard. She also knew how to lose, but in the end, would she always look back and regret turning him away?

That, finally, was the one clear answer. Of course she would.

"I might have already blown it," she whispered, cradling her head in her hands. "He's barely spoken to me since moving out."

"Because he's hurting. Lacey, I saw his face that night at the dance. I saw how it was between you. It's special. Don't throw it away out of fear. You were the one who sent him away. You've got to be the one to ask him to come back."

"How do I do that?"

Kailey finally smiled at her. "Three little words, sugar. That's all it takes."

LACEY WASN'T SURE how to get Quinn alone so they could talk. At his place, Amber would be in the way. At the ranch they ran the risk of being interrupted by Duke or one of the hands, and for this sort of conversation she wanted privacy. Time.

She finally found an opening when Carrie stopped in for tea on Thursday morning. As they chatted over chocolate chip cookies, Carrie revealed that Jack, one of the hands, was out getting his wisdom teeth pulled and that Quinn was working the horses all on his own this week. Carrie had offered to step in and take up the slack, but Duke was playing protective daddy now that she was starting to show.

So that was why he'd stayed away and not been in the office all week. Lacey was relieved it wasn't because he was avoiding her even more. The topic switched to Lacey, however, when Carrie let her know that the lawyer had called and as long as Lacey was running the office part of the ranch, the terms of the will were satisfied. Now she just had to decide if she wanted to stay on at the house or find a smaller place in town. For now, not paying rent was a good option.

It seemed like Carrie stayed and stayed and talked nonstop. Finally she left and Lacey raced to the bathroom to freshen up. She'd just go down and ask him to come to the house later when he had a break or something. She swiped on some lipstick and tidied her ponytail, swished on some mascara to brighten her eyes just a bit. Satisfied that she was acceptable, she put Ranger in his crate as a precaution against accidents, pulled on a jacket and a pair of boots and made her way to the horse barn.

The barn was warm and smelled of horses and hay, two scents that Lacey didn't find that unpleasant. Perhaps the outside of the barn looked a little neglected, but inside it was clean and tidy, with swept concrete floors and nothing piled up or lying around. She found Quinn in a stall, running his hands over the sides of a dappled mare. "Hey, there," she said softly, not wanting to startle either of them.

QUINN'S HEAD CAME up sharply at the sound of her voice. He hadn't heard her come in, but only because he'd been lost in thoughts about her again.

The past few weeks had been so weird. He'd thought by going home he'd be able to get into his old routine again. That it would feel right and this thing with Lacey wouldn't be so…present. But he'd been very, very wrong. To his surprise, home didn't quite feel like home. The new paint and floors looked different, the furniture brand-new. The bits and pieces of Marie that had been there were gone, and he realized he'd kept it exactly the same all that time in an effort to hold on to her. Like a shrine. And now it felt like he didn't belong there anymore.

He'd been living at home and wishing he was back at Crooked Valley. The only thing he'd been able to sort out for sure was that Lacey needed time and space to sort things out. He hadn't been able to move on until he was ready, and he wasn't going to push her, either. The one thing Lacey didn't expect was for him to stick around, because Carter hadn't. But Quinn could be a patient man. He hadn't given up on her yet.

And now she'd come to him. He kept his voice mellow. "What are you doing down here?"

"I came to see you. To see if we could talk."

"I'm shorthanded today." He hated to admit it, but there really wasn't a lot of spare time with Jack being out.

"I know. That's why I came to the barn."

"I don't follow." He stood and gave the mare a pat on the rump. "Good girl. You and the little one are doing fine."

The mare was expecting, and he realized that all around Lacey there was evidence of new life and reproduction and it had to be hell on her, especially when she'd wanted it so much.

"I knew you'd be alone, Quinn. I didn't want us to be overheard or interrupted. Maybe you can come to the house for a while."

"I'll try, but it might not be until later. I'm handling everything alone with Jack out today, and then I have to go get Amber." He tapped the mare's foreleg and she lifted it obligingly for him to examine the frog. He was deliberately playing it cool, but he wasn't going to be able to hold out for long. She looked so pretty, so nervous standing there fidgeting with her hands, that he really just wanted to pull her into his arms and tell her it was all going to be okay.

LACEY KNEW SHE deserved to be put off a bit. She'd been the one to close down any hope of them having a relationship. With nerves tangling over and around in her stomach, she remembered the moment he'd said he was falling in love with her.

She'd thought it impossible. A disaster…rather than a miracle. She wondered if at any time during her adulthood she'd stop being so blind.

"Just tell me what you need," he said.

Three little words. Perhaps not the three Kailey meant, but they were three that would answer his question.

"I need you."

He straightened, dropping the hoof, the mare forgotten. "What did you say?"

She wouldn't cry. She would not. Blinking furiously, she repeated the words, hope pushing against the fear in her heart. "I need you, Quinn. I can't go on this way. Nothing's right anymore."

He stepped away from the mare and came to the stall door, unlatching it and coming out into the hall, then closing it behind him again. "What are you saying, Lacey?"

She lifted her chin. "I guess I'm asking if it's too late for us."

If she expected him to fall into her arms, she was mistaken. In fact, she couldn't read his face at all, and she was suddenly very afraid that she'd missed her opportunity. That it really was too late. And she had no one to blame but herself.

"You were pretty clear a few weeks ago when you told me we were done. What changed?"

"I meant it, at the time. I'd spent a lot of energy fighting for what I wanted for years, and I lost. And then when I had something to fight for again, I was too afraid to go after it."

"And how did you come by this miraculous revelation?"

Oh, Lord, he was really holding his ground. She'd hurt him when she'd turned him away, hadn't she? And he was going to make her work now.

"Quinn," she whispered, on the verge of tears.

"You need to say it," he said firmly. "You need to, Lace."

It was time she rose to the challenge and became the kind of woman he deserved. She looked at him, standing across from her, and knew that he was right. She had to try. The idea of life without him was so utterly and completely empty.

"Kailey set me straight. She's a good friend, and happens to be pretty smart."

His face softened the tiniest bit. "Yes, she is."

And then she took a deep, fortifying breath.

"The thing is, Quinn, I was so afraid of losing you down the road that I couldn't bring myself to take a chance on us. And that wasn't giving either of us nearly enough credit." She gave a small sniff as emotion threatened to overwhelm her. "I'm miserable without you, Quinn. I miss hearing your voice telling Amber to be quiet in the morning. I miss seeing you across the dinner table. Hearing you laugh at a show on TV or talking about work even though I don't understand most of what you're saying. I love you, Quinn. I don't know how it happened, because you drive me crazy. But when you kiss me I feel alive again and when we made love I knew what it felt like to be home and it scares me to death. Scares me because I want it so much, and it's so precious and fragile and the very idea of believing in us and then possibly losing you tears me up inside. I'm afraid to have faith, Quinn. But I love you. That I can't change."

She never expected to see tears in his eyes but they were there, glistening at her as she finished her speech. His voice was raw when he replied, still standing a few feet away, not touching her, but reaching her just the same, the way he always seemed to. With his heart.

"I had faith once, too," he said hoarsely, "and had it shattered. I didn't expect to love you, either. And maybe you were right before. Maybe it's easier for me because losing Marie broke my heart, but I wasn't left, I don't know, disillusioned, like you were with Carter. There was no blame to be passed around. Just an empty hole in my life. A cloud hanging over me until you came along and brought the sun with you."

"We used to fight all the time."

"Not for long." His lips turned up just a little. "Just enough to flirt without admitting we were doing it."

He was right. They'd been playing this mating game from the start.

"Do you think we can start over?" she asked, unable to keep the thread of uncertainty out of her voice.

"I've been miserable without you," he admitted. "Amber's grouchy because she misses you, I'm grouchy because I miss you, nothing seems right. Home just isn't home anymore, Lacey. It really is where the heart is. And I'm afraid I left my heart with you."

For a man who didn't make pretty speeches, that one was pretty damned good to her mind. But she had to be absolutely sure, get everything out in the open, no surprises.

"Quinn, you know what I can and can't offer you. I understand, and want you to be a hundred percent honest."

He came forward then, put his hands on her upper arms and squeezed. "It doesn't matter that you can't have children. You, me and Amber…we can be a family. I would never, ever turn you away for that, or make you feel that you were somehow lacking. There's nothing wrong with you. Nothing except the fact that you're too damned stubborn to take a chance. I hope that's changed."

She nodded. "I have to learn to trust again somehow.

I figure a good starting point is the man I love. The most admirable man I know."

"Don't let Duke hear you say that," Quinn replied, but a smile broke out over his face. "God, it's so good to touch you again."

"Kiss me, please? I'm dying to kiss you, Quinn."

He needed no other prompting. His arms came around her as he claimed her with a kiss, his lips warm and firm and commanding. By the time they broke it off, she was quite breathless and weak-kneed.

"So we start over?" he asked hopefully.

She nodded. "We start over. We could begin with you coming to dinner with Amber tonight. I've missed her, too."

"I have to make a run home first," he said. "Say six-ish?"

"Sounds perfect."

Reluctant to let him go, she stepped into his embrace again, wrapping her arms around his ribs as she pressed her head to his chest, the rough fabric of his jacket against her cheek. "I'm sorry, Quinn. Sorry I was so stupid and scared."

"It doesn't matter," he murmured, kissing the top of her head. "You're here now. We'll make it work, Lacey. I promise."

After several long moments, the mare came to the door of the stall and stuck her head over the door, wondering what the fuss was about. Lacey laughed and Quinn lifted his hand and gave the soft muzzle a rub. "Jealous," he accused, but the lines around his face had relaxed. Lacey felt like a load had been lifted from her shoulders. That together they could do this thing.

"I'd better go decide what to make. It sucks cooking

for one." She didn't want to leave his side but knew he had work to do.

Besides, this time she knew he'd be back. With Amber and her delightful chatter. The house would be full again—full with the people she loved.

"Whatever it is, it'll be delicious. It always is."

She went to pull away but he grabbed her hand and yanked her back, quickly enough that she fell into his arms with a laugh. The laugh died, though, when he treated her to a long, lingering kiss that left her wanting all sorts of things that shouldn't happen in the middle of a horse barn.

"I love you," he murmured before letting her go.

"I love you, too," she answered.

Chapter Sixteen

For the past month, Quinn had been happier than he could ever remember being. But right now, his nerves were completely shot.

First of all, he'd had to make Amber promise to keep their secret, and he had no faith she'd be able to do so. For added security, he'd made the drive into the city and dropped her at his mother's place, which had required a quick and, he was sure, unsatisfactory explanation.

Then he'd stopped for flowers…again, in the city, because the only shop in Gibson to carry flowers was the grocery store and wouldn't that set tongues wagging? A dozen pink roses sat on the truck seat beside him. Right next to a little red envelope and a bottle of champagne.

He was so out of practice with this stuff.

Her car was in the driveway. At least that was good, because he wasn't sure what he would have done if she'd been out. Once he cut the engine, he peeked at his reflection in the rearview mirror. His brows were pulled together, forming a wrinkle at the top of his nose. He relaxed his forehead to erase it, then flicked a hand over his hair, fixing an invisible stray strand. Then he ran his finger under his collar, which felt far too tight, buttoned to the top. The knot in his tie was slightly askew, and he tried to straighten it although it refused to lie perfectly flat.

He was starting to sweat, so he figured he should get out of the truck and just get on with it.

It was ten minutes to six. The longer spring days meant that the sun still shone benevolently on the fresh grass that had greened up beautifully after the snow had melted. He left his jacket on the seat as he opened the door and then reached back for his bounty. One step after another, up the few stairs to the porch, where he hesitated.

The "rules" were that the door was unlocked between eight and six each day. But lately those rules had ceased to matter. He came and went as he pleased, stopping midday to share lunch, for coffee breaks, for dinner and movie dates. And it had been wonderful.

But it wasn't enough. So tonight he knocked on the door instead of walking right in. It seemed appropriate.

Ranger started barking his head off, the sound growing louder as the dog raced through the house to the door. Quinn could hear Lacey's voice telling him to hush, and then she opened the door.

The sight of her greeting him with a smile never failed to steal his breath.

"Quinn! I wasn't expecting you tonight."

"Surprise," he said, finding it easier than he expected to smile at her. Yeah, he was nervous, but seeing her somehow made everything all right.

"Those are for me?" she asked, her face lighting up with pleasure.

He handed her the roses. "Yes, they're for you."

"What's the occasion?"

"Do I need one?" He followed her inside and shut the

door. Tonight he'd worn his suit pants and dress shoes, not boots. When she had the flowers in her hands, she finally noticed he'd dressed up.

"Okay, now I know something's going on. Because I'm in sweats and you're all dressed up."

"I think you look beautiful." He truly did. There was something so soft and natural about her when she was like this. Her hair fell in waves over her shoulders, and he longed to sink his fingers into it and hear her say his name in that soft, husky way she did when they were alone…

But his hands were full. And there were things to say first.

"I've been doing taxes all day. I'm not wearing any makeup. You're deranged." She moved to the sink to fetch a vase and fill it with water.

"I just…I realized we never had a real Valentine's Day."

She stuck the roses in the vase and turned around, holding the vessel in her hands. "Um, really? Because I have some pretty romantic memories from Valentine's Day." She smiled at him wickedly.

"I never got you a present."

Her cheeks had turned a becoming shade of pink to match the roses and he marveled once more that he could be so lucky twice in his life. Lord, he loved her. For her kindness and her vulnerability and her strength and the way she nurtured their relationship and his family. All leading to this moment.

He stepped forward, put the champagne on the counter and took the vase from her hands. "So," he said lightly, "tonight you get champagne and flowers. You get to be treated like a princess. Oh, and Amber also realized she'd left you off her list of Valentine's card recipients and asked me to give you this."

There. That had sounded casual and breezy, right? He hoped so because his heart was pounding painfully as he handed over the little red envelope.

She took it and smiled, then her face grew puzzled. "There's something in here with the card," she said, feeling along the outside of the envelope. "I wonder what she's put in here, the sneaky thing."

She had to open it soon. He'd forgotten how to breathe.

Lacey slid her finger along the seal and opened the envelope, then pulled out the little card with her favorite Disney couple on the outside. She laughed. "Of all the fish in the sea, you're the one for me! Of course. Ariel and Eric."

She turned the card over, and he watched her face as she read the words he'd helped Amber print on the back side.

Will you marry my Daddy?

Her gaze lifted to his, surprised, confused, amazed, and he hoped beyond hope, happy. Without speaking, she reached into the envelope and took out the ring he'd purchased last week when he'd started to put this plan into motion.

Her lip started to quiver, so he stepped forward, took the ring from her fingertips and held her left hand in his own. "Lacey Duggan, will you marry me?"

At her quick nod, he slid the ring over her finger, where the diamonds winked up at them both, sealing the promise.

"Yes," she finally whispered, her voice hitching. "Oh, Quinn. It's beautiful."

"Just like you," he replied, lifting her hand and kissing her fingers. "I want us to be a family. Officially, forever. Amber already loves you like a mother and I'm wild about you. Life's too short to spend it apart. I want us to soak up every happy moment we can."

She was really crying now and he smiled indulgently, pulling her into his arms. "Shh," he soothed, cupping his hand over her head. "Today's a new start for us. I don't want you to cry. I want us to celebrate."

She stood back and swiped her fingers under her eyes. "I never thought I'd be this happy again," she replied. "It's almost too much to believe." She hesitated, like she wanted to say something but wasn't sure she should.

"What is it?" he asked, hoping she wasn't coming up with some roadblock to stand in the way of them getting married.

"It's the ranch. I know you just moved back into your house, but…" Her blue eyes pleaded with him. "I love this house. I never expected to, and it needs a family to make it a home. Would you and Amber consider moving in here?"

He barely gave it a moment's thought. Yes, he loved his house, but it was part of a past life that didn't exist anymore. He'd only kept it to give Amber some consistency, to feel like something in her life hadn't changed after her mother died. These days, when he thought of home, it was wherever Lacey was, and that meant Crooked Valley.

"If it's okay with Duke and Rylan, it's okay with me. You realize it means you're gaining one little girl and another rambunctious dog, right?"

He'd fulfilled his promise and Amber had been the

proud owner of a shepherd cross named Molly for the better part of a month.

Lacey's grin spread. "Yes, but instead of one person and one dog there'll be three people and two dogs. Better ratio, right?"

He wasn't about to argue.

They were in the middle of kissing again when the house phone rang. They were going to ignore it when Quinn realized it was his mother's number on the caller ID.

"Hello?"

"Did she say yes?"

Leave it to Amber to be impatient. "Just a minute and you can ask her yourself." He put the phone on speaker. "Okay, darlin'. Go ahead."

"Lacey?"

"Yes, Amber?"

"Are you going to be my mommy now?"

The look on Lacey's face was something he knew he'd remember forever.

"I sure am, pumpkin." She reached over and took Quinn's hand in hers. "I sure am."

* * * * *

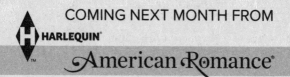
#1537 HER RODEO MAN
Reckless, Arizona • by Cathy McDavid

Confirmed bachelor and former rodeo man Ryder Beckett returns home after losing his job, only to fall for Tatum Mayweather, childhood friend, single mother...and his very off-limits coworker.

#1538 THE DOCTOR'S COWBOY
Blue Falls, Texas • by Trish Milburn

When injured bull rider Wyatt Kelley is wheeled into the ER, Dr. Chloe Brody knows she shouldn't get too attached to one of her patients. But the flirtatious cowboy has other ideas!

#1539 THE BABY BONANZA
Safe Harbor Medical • by Jacqueline Diamond

Zora Raditch's twins need a father. Lucky Mendez, her attentive housemate and a medical professional, would make a great dad. But would he want to raise another man's children?

#1540 A TEXAN FOR HIRE
Welcome to Ramblewood • by Amanda Renee

Abby Winchester is on a mission to uncover her family secrets and locate her long-lost sister. Handsome PI Clay Tanner may be just the man to help her—if he can overcome the dark secrets of his own past.

REQUEST YOUR FREE BOOKS!
2 FREE NOVELS PLUS 2 FREE GIFTS!

❖HARLEQUIN®

American ★ Romance®

LOVE, HOME & HAPPINESS

YES! Please send me 2 FREE Harlequin® American Romance® novels and my 2 FREE gifts (gifts are worth about $10). After receiving them, if I don't wish to receive any more books, I can return the shipping statement marked "cancel." If I don't cancel, I will receive 4 brand-new novels every month and be billed just $4.74 per book in the U.S. or $5.24 per book in Canada. That's a savings of at least 14% off the cover price! It's quite a bargain! Shipping and handling is just 50¢ per book in the U.S. and 75¢ per book in Canada.* I understand that accepting the 2 free books and gifts places me under no obligation to buy anything. I can always return a shipment and cancel at any time. Even if I never buy another book, the two free books and gifts are mine to keep forever.

154/354 HDN F4YN

Name _____ (PLEASE PRINT)

Address _____ Apt. #

City _____ State/Prov. _____ Zip/Postal Code

Signature (if under 18, a parent or guardian must sign)

Mail to the **Harlequin® Reader Service:**
IN U.S.A.: P.O. Box 1867, Buffalo, NY 14240-1867
IN CANADA: P.O. Box 609, Fort Erie, Ontario L2A 5X3

Want to try two free books from another line?
Call 1-800-873-8635 or visit www.ReaderService.com.

* Terms and prices subject to change without notice. Prices do not include applicable taxes. Sales tax applicable in N.Y. Canadian residents will be charged applicable taxes. Offer not valid in Quebec. This offer is limited to one order per household. Not valid for current subscribers to Harlequin American Romance books. All orders subject to credit approval. Credit or debit balances in a customer's account(s) may be offset by any other outstanding balance owed by or to the customer. Please allow 4 to 6 weeks for delivery. Offer available while quantities last.

Your Privacy—The Harlequin® Reader Service is committed to protecting your privacy. Our Privacy Policy is available online at www.ReaderService.com or upon request from the Harlequin Reader Service.

We make a portion of our mailing list available to reputable third parties that offer products we believe may interest you. If you prefer that we not exchange your name with third parties, or if you wish to clarify or modify your communication preferences, please visit us at www.ReaderService.com/consumerschoice or write to us at Harlequin Reader Service Preference Service, P.O. Box 9062, Buffalo, NY 14269. Include your complete name and address.

HAR13R

Read on for a sneak peek of
New York Times *bestselling author Cathy McDavid's*
HER RODEO MAN,
the second book of her
RECKLESS, ARIZONA *miniseries.*

Ryder stood at the pasture fence, his leather dress shoes sinking into the soft dirt. He'd have a chore cleaning them later. At the moment, he didn't care.

When, he absently wondered, was the last time he'd worn a pair of boots? Or ridden a horse, for that matter? The answer came quickly. Five years ago. He'd sworn then and there he'd never set sight on Reckless again.

Recent events had altered the circumstance of his enduring disagreement with his family. Liberty, the one most hurt by their mother's lies, had managed to make peace with both their parents. Not so Ryder. His anger had not dimmed one bit.

Was coming home a mistake? Only time would tell. In any case, he wasn't staying long.

In the pasture, a woman haltered a large black pony and led it slowly toward the gate. Ryder leaned his forearms on the top fence railing. Even at this distance, he could tell two things: the pony was severely lame, and the woman was spectacularly attractive.

The pair was a study in contrast. While the pony hobbled painfully, favoring its front left foot, the woman moved with elegance and grace, her long black hair misbehaving in the mild breeze. She stopped frequently to check on the pony, and when she did, rested her hand affectionately on its sleek neck.

Something about her struck a familiar, but elusive, chord with him. A memory teased at the fringes of his mind, just out of reach.

As he watched, the knots of tension residing in his shoulders relaxed. That was, until she changed direction and headed toward him. Then he immediately perked up, and his senses went on high alert.

"Hi," she said as she approached. "Can I help you?"

She was even prettier up close. Large, dark eyes analyzed him with unapologetic interest from a model-perfect oval face. Her full mouth stretched into a warm smile impossible not to return. The red T-shirt tucked into a pair of well-worn jeans emphasized her long legs and slim waist.

"I'm meeting someone." He didn't add that he was now ten minutes late or that the someone was, in fact, his father.

"Can I show you the way?"

"Thanks. I already know it."

"You've been here before?"

"You…could say that. But it's been a while."

Look for HER RODEO MAN by New York Times bestselling author Cathy McDavid, available March 2015 wherever Harlequin American Romance books and ebooks are sold!

www.Harlequin.com